Dukes of Hell

Book 1:

Viper

By M. Francis Lamont

This is a work of fiction. Names, characters, businesses, places, events, locales, and incidents are either the products of the author's imagination or used in a fictitious manner. Any resemblance to other works of fiction, actual persons, living or dead, or actual events is purely coincidental.

COVER CREDIT:

Photographer: *Furious Fotog*

Model: *Matthew Hosea- Inked Model*

Agency: *Monarch Management*

Cover Design: *Mama Llama Designs*

Dedicated to the memory of Blair, Ryan, and Billy, who I never did any of this with.

Thanks to B1 for the introduction, and the therapy. B2 for jumping on board with this crazy idea.

Matt and Robin for the encouragement, for understanding and for all your great contributions to the story.

My team of red pens and powerful women, I would be lost without you.

Special thanks to Craig, Darren, Randy, and the boys for the life lessons that I'll never forget. I hope you like the pie.

This book, this series, was written to pay tribute to the special group of men, gone and still here, who helped me pick myself up from the lowest of lows.

It is the best way I can think of to say thank you. After all, they say if a writer loves you, you'll live forever in their stories. So I hope they ride on forever.

Fortune Favors the Brave

1

"You're sure you understand what you're signing up for…" He picked up her ID card from the table. "Betty? This your real name and age? Are you really from RiverDell?" The burly man said, his leather vest open over a white tank top with his club 'colors' on open display for all the bar to see.

Sure, the place wasn't busy. It was Thursday before sunset. There weren't many people out to see the early show at the strip club, but there were enough people there that she felt nervous. She had heard about this chance from a friend who danced every other weekend. She had been going to take it herself, but at the last minute, she had gotten an offer to be a ring girl at a televised MMA event. It was unlike anything she had ever even considered doing before but she needed money if she was still going to have a place to live at the end of the month.

"Yeah. I mean, yes Sir. I understand that as soon as I sign that I am expected to be here tomorrow night at six, to be picked up and taken to the clubhouse, your clubhouse, for the weekend."

He nodded, flipping her ID back and forth between his fingers which drew her attention up his fully inked arms. They were filled with faces, alive and dead, plus numbers and symbols that she was sure she was never going to know what they meant and even more sure that she didn't want to know. When she looked him full in the face she would have gasped if she had been breathing up to this point. He had eyes like chocolate on a face that should have been on the cover of a magazine. His nose had been broken more than once and there was the hint of a lingering black eye, but the chiseled jawline and eye-catching lips pressed in a firm line while he continued to stare at her blankly.

"Yes. The weekend, a full forty-eight hours that you can never speak of to anyone. Ever." He slid her ID into his pocket. "It means that for those two days, we own you. There is no 'no', there is no 'stop', there is nothing we can't do as long as there's no permanent repercussions. Got it Betty?"

"Yeah. I got it. Anything else before I go home to sleep and pack?" She said, trying not to panic. Her friend would never have suggested this to her if she was going to get hurt and she was probably just going to end up cleaning up after and maybe cooking for a bunch of guys that didn't have women in their lives. They couldn't possibly be the sex-fueled, drunken party boys that they were rumored to be, could they?

"Well, now that you mention it there is one more thing, before or after you sign the paper, but we will need a private room for this." He stood, towering over her barely five-foot-tall frame. Tapping the paper, he walked past her. "I'll be in the back room, second door on the left. If you sign it, meet me there within five minutes. I'll be walking out the door in five minutes and ten seconds if you aren't there."

He walked past her, leaving Betty staring down at the paper and pen. The smell of him lingered, leather, sweat and traces of a cologne she couldn't name but it sparked an instant desire in the back of her mind. Would it really be so awful if he were as bad as it was rumored? Maybe there would be time to…there was no time. Not if she wanted to be able to pay her rent and keep the apartment that had taken her months to find.

She scribbled her signature across the piece of paper and followed the lingering hint of his cologne to the room where he was waiting. Opening the door, she found him sitting on the leather sofa, a glass of whisky in his hand, the rim of his ball cap pulled down over his eyes.

"So, you decided to sign it did you, Betty?" He asked in a low growl that carried the same disbelief of her true name as earlier.

He didn't need to know that it was her mother's name or that the ID had been created for her as a gift a few years ago, 'just in case'.

"I did and I'm ready for whatever this final test is that you needed a private room for. What do you want from me…?" She smiled and bit her lip. "I don't even know your name."

"You can call me Viper."

"Viper? What kind of name is that for a…"?

"That is the only name you need to know and it's one you'll be screaming this weekend." He set the glass down and stood, slowly stalking towards her. "Now, stop talking."

Betty stilled. The silence was so complete she could hear the ice cubes cracking in Viper's glass.

"Good girl. This is a test. To make sure that you are not going to panic this weekend and cause a scene. You need to be ready for anything at any moment." He circled, coming close behind her. "You need to be willing for anything."

"I will. There's not any choice there."

"Smart, though disobedient." He surprised her with a swift slap to her ass. "Quiet. Strip. I want to see what we're playing with this weekend so I can plan a few…games."

She could feel his nearness as she stepped out of her heels and started to undo her jeans. The sharp inhale when she unsnapped her top to expose the white lace of her new bra made her pause, slowly dropping the cotton to the floor beside her black pumps.

“Well now. Those are worth seeing.” He said over her shoulder. Sliding his hand around her waist to roughly tug the zipper down on her jeans revealing the bow at the top of the matching French cut shorts. “So are those. Get the jeans out of the way and put your heels back on.”

She shivered and, with a slow exhale pushed the hip-huggers to the floor and stepped back into the black leather heels. Closing her eyes, she let her hands hang by her side, waiting for his instructions, barely able to breathe.

“You are a natural. Obedient and…” He slipped his hand down the front of her panties, stroking the tip of his finger down her clit. Her entire body tensed as he teased around her entrance, circling, and stroking until she was clenched, wet and needy for more. “Eager. I think you need this. I think you need a weekend of fucking. Hard, fast and with the variety of a dozen cocks everywhere we can fit ‘em. Don’t you, Betty baby.”

She gasped when he suddenly slid his free hand to bend her over at the waist as he pressed his middle finger deep into her core. Pressing his hardened erection tight against her ass, the hand that wasn’t finger fucking her slipped up to grip her lace covered breasts, kneading with a bruising strength. He started to imitate a fierce, possessive, pounding from behind her. Sending a tremor through her that threatened to throw her off her feet.

“Don’t fall Baby. If you fall, I’m gonna pull you to your knees and feed my cock through those pretty lips.” He growled, adding a second finger to his strokes. “I don’t plan on that tonight so don’t disappoint me.”

Betty thought she was going to scream as he coaxed her body over the edge. She wanted more of this, more of him. If his voice didn’t carry a note of anger, she would have fallen on purpose just to have the chance at his cock. Her body started to shake, and he pressed his thumb to her clit.

“Oh…God.” She tossed her head back as her body clenched around him and her hips pressed back against him as he stilled his own.

“Good girl, but there is no God where you’re going. If you respond like this to a simple little test you are going to be so much fun this weekend.”

A blush on her cheeks, Betty turned to face him with a smile. “As long as I get to be with you then I know it’ll be a great time.”

"Just remember. I'm not going to fall in love with you. No one out here is. I'm going to fuck you, hard, fast, and often. I'll be holding you down for my friends to fuck you, then I'll fuck you with them. Understand? This isn't love. This is fucking because that's what you're there for. That's what you're signing up for, two days of near constant sex. We even have a few that will want to fuck you while you sleep. Not me though. You'll be awake and aware every time I use you, and Betty?"

"Yes Viper?"

"I'm going to use you a lot."

2

Betty left the strip club feeling excited about the weekend at the sexual mercy, or lack thereof, of Viper, but after a fitful night's sleep she was starting to lose her nerve. Packing her bag while sipping a cup of coffee she was starting to worry. At first it was concern that her lingerie collection wasn't going to be as inspiring as it has seemed in her head. Then she began to wonder about Viper himself, which led to wondering what the other men were like and how many of them there would be. It quickly snowballed into her nearly dialing to cancel a few times, but when she thought of those rough, calloused hands on her again she knew she had to go through with it.

When her bag was packed and next to the door, she attacked her closet to try and decide what to wear. She had enough experience with dressing for dates but what should she wear to be fucked by at least a half dozen biker men? Would it matter? Or would whatever she was wearing be removed within minutes of her arrival? She decided on something that would be considered 'sweet and innocent'. A thigh length blue cotton dress with a deep v neckline and thin shoulder straps, with her hair in a high ponytail, and a pair of shiny black strappy sandals.

At half past five she grabbed her jacket and the small bag then headed out the door to make sure that she arrived at the club on time for the pick-up. She arrived early enough to take a seat, order a drink to calm her nerves, and watch the door for the arrival of her ride. Even though he had said it would be someone else, Betty hoped that Viper would be the one to drive her. The thought of being alone with him in the small space of a car was exciting but as she slammed back the final splash of her gin and tonic, she was disappointed to see another man wearing the same vest with badges that Viper had worn strut into the bar and scan the room for her. He looked from her to his hand, then walked up to her, she guessed that he was holding her ID.

"You Betty?" She nodded, breathless with the realization that this was really happening. Her last chance to run was gone when he grabbed her bag from the seat next to her and jerked his thumb towards the door. "Let's get going. Don't want to be late when there's people waiting for you."

“How many people?” She asked once they were outside and headed towards a dirty jeep that was covered in so much mud that she couldn’t even tell what color it was.

“More than some, less than a lot.” He said cryptically as he opened the door and tossed her bag on the seat in the back. “Get on in. You’re the last member of the party and Viper is waiting for us at the clubhouse, well waiting for you."

"He's waiting for me?" She said, unable to hide the smile that betrayed her growing crush on the dangerous man.

"He's not the only one, but it was his job to find the girl for this weekend and a lot is riding on how well you do." Her driver said with a smirk, as if he knew what she was thinking or at least who she was thinking of. "If you screw up, he's the one that will catch it. So, you really should be the good girl he said you are." He looked sideways at her and gave a hiss of appreciation. "He said you were exceptionally good. I'm looking forward to seeing just how true that is."

"Will you? Are you someone that I'll be…with?" She asked nervously as his hand moved to rest on her thigh. He didn't move it higher or knead the exposed flesh but just let it rest as he drove them out of the city and down a few twisting dirt roads, filled with as many exits as there were potholes.

"Honey, the closest I am going to get to having a chance at you is from the far side of the bar unless I get special permission. I am sure going to enjoy the show though. Do me a favor and make it a good one will ya?" He said with a chuckle as they crossed a bridge and entered a yard surrounded by a brick wall and a forest of trees so thick Betty couldn't see through them. "Here we are and there is Viper standing by the back door. Looks like the it's time for your curtain call Betty. Break a leg, not your heart, kid." He said, handing her bag to her and stopping just a few feet away from the door.

His arms were crossed over his chest and a finger tapped impatiently. Betty couldn't help but be in awe of the impressive figure he cut as rain started to fall from the darkening sky. "I'm not late, am I?" She asked, slowly walking towards him as his eyes roamed over her from the ground up to her face.

"Not yet. Come on, I don't want that to change." He said with a hint of a drawl that she hadn't noticed when he had spoken to her in the bar.

"Come on Betty Baby." Viper said, ushering her into the kitchen where a few guys in their twenties were working on trays of food. "We've got to get you dressed."

"I wasn't sure what to wear so I brought some stuff with me if this isn't the kind of thing you wanted. I forgot to ask." She was nervous and rambling a little bit, but he just smiled and shook his head.

"You're fine. Just a little overdressed." Unlocking a door, he handed her a key. "If I tell you to go, this is where you come and lock it behind you. If it gets... rowdy or cops raid the house, you come here and lock the door. They'll know that you're a guest not involved in club business if you're in here. Understand?" He asked, staring her in the eyes until she nodded.

She still couldn't believe that she was going to spend the weekend having sex with random guys whose names she probably wouldn't even know. "I understand. Just a little bit nervous."

"No one is going to hurt you. This is fun, a party. You can let go of every inhibition you ever had and enjoy the sex. Just don't get sloppy drunk though. Drinks are on the house, anything you want, just stay awake and aware, alright?" He opened the blinds and the room filled with grey light from outside.

"I've never been a drinker, but I'll remember that. Something to help me relax would be great though." She paused, fidgeting nervously "So what am I supposed to wear? Since you said this is too much?"

He walked around her slowly before opening the closet. "Take everything but the heels off. I'm going to show you off to the members and we'll go from there."

She had stripped off the dress and tucked it into her bag which seemed almost pointless now and was standing in a matching sky-blue lace bra and thong set.

He checked his phone when it buzzed then turned from the closet, tossing what looked like a few scraps of fabric to the double bed.

"I said all of it and I don't have time for you to be shy about it. I need to have you on the tray in the kitchen in less than five minutes." He spun her around and undid her bra, sliding his hands forward to cup her breasts, kneading them as he bit the side of her neck with a growl. "Damn I can't wait for my turn with you." His hands slid down to hook his thumbs in the waistband of her panties and wrenched them down past her knees. "Step out of those and follow me. Let's get this party started."

Completely naked Betty followed Viper back out of the room and down the narrow stairs to the kitchen where every man in the room turned to stare at her.

"Up on those boards Betty. The boys are going to put the food around you then I'll be putting a few things right on you to make the presentation perfect." Viper grinned at her. "They're going to be floored to see you like this. No one has ever done anything more than lead the girl into the room and just let them look. This is going to be amazing."

He looked so happy that Betty couldn't help but return his smile as the other men decorated her table and Viper placed a strawberry surrounded by cherries between her legs to cover her and pineapple rings around each nipple. It felt like something out of a movie and she struggled not to squirm and disrupt the placement.

"It's tempting to put something into your mouth too, but I think that might be one step too far. Besides I'm sure that'll happen soon enough anyway." He excitedly placed a kiss on her forehead and signaled for the others to roll the table through the double doors after him.

She was excited as voices buzzed around for a moment before going completely silent when they realized she was there. It was impossible to turn her head, but she could hear heavy booted feet getting closer until the table was surrounded. Then they began to talk.

"Well now, that is a dinner I could eat all night."

"Damn Viper. Boy, when you said you were bringing dessert, I didn't think it would be that good."

"When dinner is done, I am going to enjoy burning off some calories."

The other comments were similar and grew more eager and complimentary as the men ate the food from the plates around her. No one ate the fruit decorating her, but a few members brushed their fingers curiously against her.

"So, what are we going to do with this tasty little piece and when do we get the cream to go with those strawberries?"

She couldn't see the face of the man talking but she felt a large, solid hand rest at the top of her thigh, his fingers sliding slowly towards the fruit covering her. She looked up, waiting for something to happen. The face of the man whose hand that was now exploring her exposed body slid into view, and though he wasn't Viper, he was stunningly handsome with a chiseled jaw and bright blue eyes that were hungry. She recognized what he was hungry for and gave him an encouraging smile.

"Why not let me get her cleaned and upright so you can appreciate every curve she's got. Trust me, if you think she looks good on her back, you should see her when she's bent over. It's a beautiful sight."

The men laughed appreciatively, and Betty blushed a little at the crude praise.

"No sense wasting that sweet fruit laying on her tits." Said a voice she hadn't heard yet. Before she could look around and try to catch a glimpse of the speaker one of the pineapple rings was lifted from her breast and a mouth took its place. The bristle of a mustache and beard tickled her for a second before she felt the heated moisture of a mouth, sucking and licking the juices left behind by the fruit. Another hand caressed the other breast and once the pineapple had been removed, she felt the lick of a pierced tongue circling her nipple before slowly drawing it in between teeth that scraped just enough to make her whimper. The sound she made worked like a signal of acceptance for the men around her to begin their exploration of her body.

Soon there were hands all over her body, touching her, kneading her breasts, and threading into her hair. Her legs were pulled open, firmly but gently. The cherries that had been piled over her pussy fell between them, but the strawberry was held in place by a warm hand. The large berry began to circle and tease at her entrance while one of the smooth cherries pressed and teased her clit. The pressure and the tickle of the stem had her squirming and shifting her hips against the strawberry that was being pressed, carefully inside her. The speared tip was as firm as a cock and she opened herself to the invasion with a moan that earned her a grunt of satisfaction from the man that was playing with her.

"Looks as though she's as eager to be played with as we are to play." A deep voice said, as the fruit was removed, and Viper pulled her upright to sit. She looked around for the first time with curiosity and wonder. When she saw the giant of a man that was eating the strawberry, her juices glistening on the bright red meat of the fruit, her jaw dropped in surprise. He was terrifying and mesmerizing in the same breath, with a dark beard and long untied hair past his shoulders. The plain white tank top and jeans, instead of the vest like several others were wearing, made the bulk of him even more impressive. The straining denim below his belt buckle made her think that every part of him was bigger than anything she had ever had before.

"Don't know if you can fit that thing of yours in that sweet mouth Ox." One of the other men said with a laugh as Betty stared. "But I'll start the pool to see how many inches you can fit before she taps out."

Others around the room started calling out numbers and taking bets while Betty's eyes stayed glued on the stunning giant of a man that was still, slowly, eating the strawberry with a devious smile on his face. He probably knew exactly what she was thinking; she didn't care about the bets, she just wanted to see how much of him she could take.

"Well before Ox starts doing his own strip show I think I'll get little Betty here washed off and dressed in something just a little more fun." Viper said, taking her hand as he helped her off the table and pulled her towards the door to the kitchen.

Once they were through the door Viper spun and kissed her firmly, slipping a pair of fingers between her legs to press at her g-spot and give her a nearly instant orgasm with insane skill. She almost collapsed in his arms, but he caught her and whispered in her ear. “Good girl. Damn you’re a good girl. Let’s get you ready for the real thing now. Upstairs before I slap that ass again.”

3

Betty found the thrill of Viper's approval to be as motivating as his way of rewarding her. She wasn't sure what was more intoxicating; his kiss or the way he knew how to bring her to her knees in such an intense way. The way he had beamed at her was heart-stopping and if he hadn't told her that there was no chance for them, she would have thought that he wanted her as much as she wanted him. When would he have her? She could hear his voice as he said, "I'm going to use you a lot." And was so sure that he meant it, but when?

"Alright babe, time for a costume change." Viper said, rubbing his hands together before starting to rummage through the pile of fabric and accessories on the bed.

"What kind of thing are you putting me in?" Betty asked, going to the sink to wash off the residue from the fruit and touches from the men downstairs.

"Nothing much. I don't think they're ready to see you as an innocent, though maybe in the morning…yeah tomorrow we'll do you up in something so sweet it'll hurt their teeth, and the balls of any man who can't have you. Tonight though, I want them to see a sex pot, born and bread for satisfaction."

"If you think that will go over best then I trust you." Betty said, brushing her hair and pulling it into a high ponytail.

He straightened from the bed holding a red and black micro skirt, and a black sheer bra that would tie under her breasts, pushing them up perfectly.

“You shouldn’t do that.” He said roughly, tossing the clothes towards her and reaching for stockings and shoes with all the finesse of a mechanic tossing scraps around. “You’re no one’s girl here, just the party favor like I told you. Don’t start developing feelings where you shouldn’t.”

Blinking away the sting of renewed rejection she gave him a smirk and reached for a dark cherry red lipstick. “Trusting you to pick out something that you’ll want to fuck me in and trusting you with my heart are two different things Viper. Don’t get confused yourself.”

He laughed and she felt like her heart stopped.

“You have sass, I like it, but keep it in check downstairs. They’ll want fire in you eyes and hips not your mouth.” He sauntered over to her, dangling a pair of shiny black heels on his fingers. “Be a good girl for the senior members you’re about to meet and I’ll give you something I know you want.”

"What is it you think I want, Viper?" She asked, adjusting herself in the bra. If he was going to keep on teasing her then rejecting her, she was going to play as though the attraction was in his head, not hers. He could never know how bad she wanted him.

She reached out to grab his belt for balance so she could fix the strap on her shoe. She smiled to herself when her grip on his buckle let her feel just how much his body wanted her, even if his mind didn't want to admit it. He had to be close to the same size as the giant downstairs they called Ox. Thinking of him brought her mind back to the moment and the party.

"Ox is waiting, with the others, we should get back don't you think?" She walked past him to the door, secretly grinning when she saw a quick flash of anger that she wanted to see the other man so eagerly.

"You eager to settle that bet downstairs?" Viper growled, stepping between her and the door. "Just remember when you're choking on him that I can make you cum with just a touch. He doesn't have that skill."

His hand teased at the bottom of her skirt and Betty wondered if he was going to repeat what he had done in the kitchen, but he simply gave her a firm slap between the legs and let her pass.

"Remember what I said, show the members that you're everything they want you to be and I'll give you the reward we both know you want from me." Was all he said after they descended the stairs and she stood in front of the kitchen door again, just a little shaky in her high heels.

"You still haven't said what that is." She whispered to him just before he opened the door and led her out in the room that she could finally see for the first time.

There was a dance stage with a pole and a pool table on one level, doors that looked like they led to bathrooms and another, small door with a series of locks that she was guessing was some kind of office. Down the steps a half dozen men, including Ox, were waiting, staring at her like a pack of wolves. She paused at the top of the stairs, she could see there was a bar with stools and an area with a few tables.

"No second thoughts, right Betty." Viper murmured to her as he took her hand and led her down the stairs, the challenge evident in his eyes. "Just enjoy the moment and we will all have fun, lots and lots of fun."

Looking him straight in the eye then turning to look at the other men waiting for her to be among them, she responded. "No second thoughts. I was just letting everyone get an eye full before their hands are full." She stepped towards the older man in the middle of the group. He had a silver beard and dark eyes that were commanding without having to say a word. "You're the man in charge, right? I'm Betty."

“Well, Betty, you can call me Blades. You’re right about me being in charge.” He unrolled a thick black collar and curled his finger, calling her towards him. “That means I get you first. On you knees baby girl and we’ll get this party started.”

4

When Betty lowered herself to her knees in front of Blades, Viper's shaft hardened to a painful pressure. He would stand and watch Blades and the others do what they wanted to her and not say a thing. That's what she was here for, but he wanted her as badly as he knew she wanted him. He should have taken her first, in the bar when she stripped so perfectly for him, but he couldn't go back now.

She wanted him and he knew it, he found out too late, but he knew it. Not many women responded like she did to the roughness that he liked but her eyes had lit up like fireworks every time he touched her, or almost touched her. Watching her on her knees in front of Blades he felt a strange blend of pride in her performance and jealousy that it wasn't him.

The collar around her neck was thick and tight but it looked so good. He wanted to see her dressed as a pet, the collar wasn't enough, he wanted to see a tail hanging out from her ass cheeks down to the floor. He was lost in the erotic daydream for a moment but Ox's hand on his shoulder brought him back to the present just in time to see Blade thrust his naked cock through Betty's cherry red lips with a grunt of satisfaction that every man in the circle shared.

The look on Blade's face as he thrust into her mouth made

Viper's balls ache, eager for the chance he knew he would get, when it was his turn. The other members unfastened their jeans and got ready for their turn to initiate the party favor. Every member was ready for her, their cocks hard and ready, a few glistening with drops of pre-cum as they stroked in anticipation. He refused to do the same though, he was as eager for the touch of her tongue as the rest of them.

Blades stopped thrusting into Betty's open and eager mouth and used her ponytail to turn her to his lieutenant, Dagger, for the next turn. The light in her eyes and enthusiastic smile on her face before she wrapped those cherry lips around Dagger gave Viper a sense accomplishment. He had chosen a girl who was doing so well with what would frighten more girls than it would excite. Dagger didn't last as long as Blades and Viper debated if he wanted to be before or after Ox, who was so excited he was practically bouncing on the balls of his feet. The big man thought that he was going to be the biggest and best performance of this circle. They were competitive, each man wanted to last the longest or have Betty respond more for them than the rest. With a smirk Viper moved to the last position, he knew that she would be her best for him. He watched the repeat performance with Rex and Doc before it was time for Ox.

When Ox stepped up to Betty with a grin that could only be described as viciously enthusiastic Viper had to stop his fists from clenching. They had competed for position within the club and Ox thought his size was going to make the difference, but Viper knew he was smarter and willing to go as far as the club needed him to go. The Dukes of Hell Club would find out soon enough that Viper would not hesitate to strike or make sacrifices for the club and that Ox was only doing what it took to be able to enjoy the benefits, like Betty, nothing more.

Her lips stretched around him as he pressed forward, thrusting his hips hard when she hesitated. Her eyes bulged as her mouth was filled with the throbbing man meat. She wasn't going to be able to take it all unless she could fight the panic and Ox wasn't going to give her the chance. He gripped the base of her ponytail and forced another inch down her throat, not caring that her entire body stiffened, and her eyes flashed with a second of fear as she tried to breath around his shaft.

"Ox! Enough." Blades called, with a smirk just before Viper was about to step in and stop the bigger man. "She can't take all that man." He continued, clapping Ox on the shoulder. "Let her breathe."

"She did better than most." Ox laughed and leaned down

to kiss Betty, patting her cheek afterwards. “You did good. We’ll try again later. Hmm pet?”

Viper wanted to laugh almost as much as he wanted to see how many of Ox’s teeth he could knock out before someone stopped him. If he had taken his time then she could have taken more, she would for Viper, he was certain of it. There was only one man between Ox and Viper, and he knew that Dev wouldn’t last long under the pressure of everyone’s eyes being on him added to the knowledge that he was Ox’s follow up act. His cock slipping between the cherry red lips was so erratic and fast that Viper wanted to yell for him to finish. He couldn’t wait show them what Betty could really do when the shaft between her lips belonged to a real man, one that knew how to fuck any hole a woman wanted.

Dev had a sudden and sloppy finish, but Betty handled it like the pro Viper knew she wasn’t. Everything he had found out about her since she signed the contract told him that she had never done anything even close to this before. She wasn’t innocent, he wouldn’t have brought her here if she were, but she wasn’t one of the girls that sought out this kind of life and she didn’t do drugs or owe anyone but the government anything.

“Viper. Hey man, you’re up, if you’re actually gonna play this time.” Ox laughed, clapping him on the shoulder.

"I think I will. Someone has to show you how to feed a cock to a pretty girl. It's all about control." He almost never played a part in this kind of party but with Betty he couldn't help himself.

"Controlling her or yourself?" Dev asked after cleaning up and yanking his jeans up around his hips.

"It's a blend of both." He said, stroking her cheek after stepping up to where she was kneeling on the floor. "She wants to be controlled but doesn't know it yet. It is up to the man to show her what she wants. If you do it right, then she will be dripping and ready for you by the time you're ready to blow your load."

Ignoring the questions that the others were grumbling at each other he brushed the back of his knuckles across her soft pale cheek. Taking her chin between his thumb and forefinger Viper smiled deviously when her lips parted, and her eyes flicked up to his. The anticipation was building in his body, but he wasn't ready to give her what she wanted just yet.

"Let's just make this a little easier for you." He said reaching to slide the bra straps from her shoulders and leaning over her to unfasten the band. She nuzzled against the crotch of his jeans where his cock was straining for release and relief. "Much better, hmm?" He smiled as her nipples puckered from the cool air. The men around him murmured enthusiastically. “To prove a point to anyone who doubts, have I fed you my shaft before?” He asked, his eyes moving from Blades to Ox.

“No, you haven’t.” She answered, and when he arched a brow she added. “Sir.”

“Open those cherry lips and show me how much you want this?” Viper said with a grin, trying to hold back a burst of pride in his personal victory. When she dropped her jaw open, her eyes locked to his while she waited with an eagerness in her eyes for him to tug his jeans and shorts down enough to let his cock free.

It was bliss when she rose higher on her knees to catch him, letting him slide into the heat of her mouth with an ease none of the others had experienced. She was trying to swallow him whole, milking him with her mouth while he slowly built a rocking pace with his hips.

“Take it all babe. To the base.” He said gruffly, his voice straining, his body fighting to maintain control over his arousal. Her mouth on his cock was better than he had anticipated. The soft smooth pull of her lips on his shaft, with her tongue stroking the vein throbbing on the bottom of his rod. She was making sure that he was going to have to fight for his power and his pride. She had already taken more of him in than she had of Ox and so when her nose pressed deep into his short and curlies he was ready to let go and shoot a load deep down her hot and welcoming throat. Her eyes were begging him for it and his hand smoothly rose from her shoulder, up the back of her neck to grip the base of that waving ponytail. His lower jaw tensed, and his ass clenched as he got ready to let go. The moment was destroyed at the last second when the worst voice he could have heard called from the door.

"Let her have it, Viper. Let's see my baby brother feed it to her and get the party started."

"Fuckin' shit." Viper hissed and pulled abruptly out of Betty's mouth, hiding his grin when he caught the sound of her whimper of disappointment. "Loch? What in the blazes of hell are you doing here? You're supposed to be in LA."

"When I heard there was a good, old fashioned, Dukes party going on I couldn't miss it, or the pretty little party favor Ox texted me a picture of when you showed off her ID." Loch said with a laugh as he dumped his bag and helmet in a chair. "I only wish I got here before the introductions had been made. I'll have to have a shower before I join in the fun." He looked from Viper, who was trying to decide if he would hug him or hammer him, then to Betty. "You wanna join me sweetness? Or does baby brother have plans for you already?"

“Oh, shut up, you gobshite” Viper said with a laugh.

Betty stood slowly. Her shoulder bumped Viper as though she was looking to him for protection. It seemed she was more uncertain of Loch than she was of the other guys. It had to be his brother that threw a wrench in things.

“No woman wants to wash the stench off of you, ya bastard.” Blades called from the bar with a laugh. “Besides, you’re late. No special privileges or private time. Viper get her cleaned up and ready to go. I’ve got an appetite that has nothing to do with the grill.”

5

"You didn't get to finish." Betty said, turning to look at Viper as soon as they were in the kitchen. "Do you want to? Before you take me back there?"

"You're saying you want me to?" Viper replied, arching a brow at her.

He was making her feel a little nervous about the request. She didn't know if she wanted it because it wasn't fair to him that the other man had interrupted or because she wanted him to experience the moment of orgasm because of her attention.

"I'm just saying that you, well you didn't, and you were going to, and that guy interrupted us." She stammered, suddenly feeling the weight of his words in her gut; 'This isn't love, this is fucking.' She took a step towards the stairs to her room. "Never mind Viper. I'll just go upstairs and wash up."

She kicked off the heels and ran upstairs with them in her hand. This was the most bizarre day of her life. She had already been intimate with more men in the last hour than she had in the last five years before that. It was an amazing rush to feel desired by six men that should have terrified her but instead each seemed more muscular and gorgeous than the last. Blades and Dagger might be a bit older than the rest of the club members, but Ox and Loch were mesmerizing.

Ox was a mountain of a man in every way she could think of, her jaw still ached from trying to wrap her mouth around him but his smile and the way his dark eyes lit up had made that moment something she would be proud of, even if she never told a soul about this weekend. The way he looked in his jeans and tank top with muscles that rippled with each move of his arms made her excited to see what would happen in a one on one encounter. Would he be rough and exciting or surprisingly gentle?

"Did anyone say you could touch yourself?" Barked Viper from the door.

Betty looked over at him and then in the mirror where she saw her hand teasing the edge of her skirt with her subconscious need for pleasure after the men had gotten off all around her.

"No one said I couldn't." She replied, locking her eyes to his as she slowly slid the skirt down over her hips and let it fall to the floor. He was still holding the bra she had been wearing when she went downstairs in his tightly clenched fist. Did the thought of her pleasing herself piss him off that much or was he wondering who she was thinking of? Deciding to play it a little dangerous she sat on the bed and slid off the heels, all while keeping her eyes locked to the deep brown ones staring at her.

"It was hot, downstairs. Every one of them wanted more than my mouth, didn't they? It's what you wanted, for Blades and Dev to want me? Dagger too?" His eyes got bigger with each name she mentioned, and she wanted to smile. She circled her finger in a spiral from her belly button downwards and his eyes followed hungrily. "Ox would have taken me right there if someone said he could, don't you think? I did what you wanted so can't I have a little release if I make it quick?"

He threw the bra onto the floor and stalked across the room to her, the denim of his jeans straining to release him. Betty wet her lips and began to reach for his belt when he caught her wrists in one and placed the other on her shoulder.

"You want pleasure? Lay back."

He wasn't asking, he was telling, and she had to obey because his hand was resting between her breasts and holding her down where he wanted her as he positioned himself between her legs. Betty was trembling with anticipation when he began to press kisses over her stomach and down towards where she was aching for his touch to send her over the edge of bliss.

"You are so fucking pretty Betty, right here."

He pressed his thumb against her clit, chuckling as she bucked her hips, needing more. She was starting to think he was going to torture by leaving her on the edge of release but when he sank to his knees, a hand holding her still by playing with her breasts, she began to hope he might mean what he said. When his finger started to circle her hole she thought he was going to used those skilled digits to bring her over the edge like he had in the kitchen but with her eyes closed in anticipation she got the surprise of the night: his tongue.

He was going to, oh gods he was already, licking and sucking her pussy as though he was starved and there was no other meal in site. She couldn't help herself from bucking against his mouth. When his tongue stiffened into a spear-tip, thrusting into her hot wet core she was practically howling with the pleasure he was giving. Her body tightened and she gripped the sheets of the bed with both fists, she wanted to let go, to give in to the sensation, but she couldn't. If she did that then he would stop, and they would go back downstairs, back to the sexy games he had devised for her.

"Don't fight me Betty. You know I'll get what I want even if you don't." He hummed against her, making it even harder not to give in.

"Viper, please? Just a little more?" She whimpered, unable to stop herself from begging. She could feel him smile against her. He knew that he had won, that she wanted him more than the others, he could probably guess all the other things she wanted from him as well and why she had offered to finish the blow job his brother had interrupted.

With one last broad lick of his tongue against her pussy Viper moved above her. His fingers speared her so suddenly that she had no time to prepare herself. Her back arched and she let go of the sheets to reach for his jeans frantically. If he could make her wet by using it on her mouth, he had to be even better between her legs.

"Fuck me Viper, now! Before we go back down there and everyone else gets to play with me."

His fingers didn't stop, and she was tremblingly close to orgasm, but he pulled his hips away from her hands.

"Not yet babe. You'll get that when I say so. Remember who's the boss here." He said with a devilish smirk as he curled his fingers. "Now, you're going to cum for me and then we'll play a little bit of dress-up for the boys downstairs."

He was good and she couldn't help it, when his eyes locked to hers and his thumb pressed against her clit, she coasted over the edge of bliss and her head rolled back as every tightened muscle in her body released. Clenching around his fingers she cried out his name in the moment of her orgasm.

"Good girl, Betty." He chuckled and gave her a sharp slap between her legs to sit her up. "Now, get up. I have something a little fun for you to put on."

"What? You're not going to…I thought you would. Don't you want to have actual sex with me Viper?" She asked, frustrated even though her body was still shaking from the strength of the pleasure he'd given her. "I thought you did. I could have sworn."

"Don't get any ideas about me Betty. Don't think of me at all." He said gruffly.

His hand was full of a gauzy material and some delicate looking chains. She wasn't sure but she was fairly certain that his hand was shaking slightly. Was he that angry at her for suggesting that he wanted more, or did he want her that badly?

"Why not Viper?" She stood up and stepped over to him, daring him to ignore her nudity and the flush on her entire body from what he had done. "Don't lie to me. I can see how pitched that tent in your jeans is so you can't say you don't want me. So why not? That's why I'm here, isn't it?"

"Why you're here is because the club is paying you to fuck

and be fucked by the members." He growled. "Not by me just because I got a hard on when I look at you."

He straightened the gauzy fabric between his hands with a smile and an arched brow. It reminded her of something a harem girl would wear in one of those cheesy old movies.

"You're not serious with that are you? A slave girl? Isn't that a bit cliché under the circumstances?" She rolled her eyes at him, which made him hole up the other hand, which held a delicate, sparkling chain. "Viper?"

"Let's get you dressed Betty baby." He smirked. "You're gonna make a few wet dreams come true in this little get up. Blades likes a little hint of the exotic."

"Well then let's get to work. I wouldn't want to disappoint him." She smiled then had a devious thought. "What about Loch? What does he like?"

Her guess that there was a rivalry between the brothers was confirmed when his eyes darkened.

"Loch likes strippers and porn stars. He's got no interest in a sweet little thing like you. He'll play the games and might even take a turn with you, but trust me sweetheart, you're not his type either."

"Because you say or because he says so?" She asked, trying to keep her voice innocent while she wrapped the second piece of gauze into a halter top. She was amazed at how sheer the material was.

“Because that’s how it is.” He replied, picking up a pair of rubber tipped nipple clamps with chimes lining the chain between them. “The boys are gonna love this. They’re gonna tug on this chain so try not to resist too much.”

“What if I want them to pull me around a little bit?” She asked, playing with the chimes.

“Then be careful what you wish for. Once the fucking starts down there it’s going to keep going. Every one of us will be expected to put our cocks in you somewhere. You’ll get your wish to have mine, not the way I’d give it to you if we were alone, but it’s the first night of the party and everyone is geared up and wants to play with every part of you they can get a hand on. This is it.”

He took the chain in his hand and tugged just hard enough to cause her to fall against him, his hand raised so her breast landed in his palm. He tugged at the collar until she was close enough to kiss. It was rough, not a drop of tenderness but with a mutual yearning that was felt in every stroke of their tongues against each other and the powerful grip he kept on her breast, kneading it so hard Betty wondered if it would bruise and if he meant for it to mark her, even if it was just for himself. What would it take for him to admit that he wanted her for more than this?

He broke the kiss, leaving her breathless and needy all over again.

“Alright, Betty. It’s showtime. Make me proud.”

6

When they came back into the main room of the clubhouse Betty's appearance was greeted by howls and whistles from the members and Viper smirked as he spun her to showcase just how well decked out she was in the ridiculous fantasy costume. He like his women naked, though he was never opposed to a full dressed quickie, in the car, a restaurant bathroom and a few other places. He wasn't a man for playing dress up with a sex partner. Until now.

Betty was soaking up the attention as though she was starving for it, as if he hadn't just given her a mind-blowing orgasm upstairs, followed by a kiss. He could smell how aroused she was by it. She wanted him. He wanted to laugh at how angry she was that he didn't fuck her upstairs. She thought he didn't want her when all he was doing was following rules. If he brought 'sloppy seconds' down to the senior men, it would be worse than if he hadn't brought a girl at all. As soon as things got going, really going, he would get to make good on his promise to use her and use her well. She would know, without a doubt, that he and his cock wanted as much of her as he could get. Loch and the others be damned, he would make sure that she wanted him and only him when this was done.

“Viper, brother, you did good. The girl looks good enough to eat.” Blades called, patting his leg for Betty to come sit on him, which she did. Viper watched her sashay her perfectly rounded ass over to sit on the senior member’s leg.

At forty-two Blades wasn’t as old as he seemed next to the twenty-six-year-old but when his lips touched the skin of her neck and his hand slid across her tanned stomach Viper thought he was going to scream. To save his sanity and his life Viper went behind the bar and started mixing the drink orders that were waiting as everyone gathered around Betty.

“Pussy hungry wolves.” He grumbled, pouring whiskey into a trio of tumblers, and sliding them across the bar to his brother. “You’re not circling with the rest of them?” He asked, handing him a beer.

“Nah. Not yet. Watching you squirm in your shorts is more fun, though it looks like it’s going to get a lot more interesting.” Loch pointed his beer towards where one Blades’ hands were between Betty’s legs and the other was undoing the fly on his jeans. “You know once he does her then she’s fair game for the rest of us, including you and me, right?”

“Oh yeah. I know. I’ve been waiting on it, though, upstairs she was begging for me. I had to follow the rules though, of course.” Viper said with a shrug and a shot of tequila.

“Oh. Right, the rules. That’s why you didn’t and why you’re looking at her as though she’s a piece of prime rib.”

Viper shrugged, his eyes not leaving Betty as Blades guided her to mount his bared cock. He couldn’t see her face but the look on the member’s face told him that Betty had to feel as good as he thought. He would make sure that he could see her face each time he fucked her, he wanted to watch her eyes roll back as she came and see the sweat beading on her breasts as she bounced on his shaft. She was working hard on Blades. The older man was either a lazy fuck or he just liked to watch the girl work for it, and she was giving a great show.

The chimes that were strung between her tits were singing as she bucked and writhed in Blades’ lap. When the chair spun so she was facing the bar Viper could see that she wasn’t having as much fun as she had when he had his mouth, or even his fingers, on her sex.

“See.” Loch said with a smirk, taking a deep drink. “She’s watching you, little brother. Someone has a crush on the ‘big bad biker’.” He laughed and put the empty beer bottle on the bar. “Another one and a shot for you so you can make it through until you get a go at her. Maybe once you scratch the itch it won’t bother you so badly.”

“Yeah. Maybe that’s what I need. To scratch an itch.” He slammed back another tequila shot as Blades buried his face between Betty's tits and shot his load inside her with a laugh. Betty had barely stood from the stool when Dagger gripped her hips and bent her over, ramming himself deep inside with a single thrust while the others cheered and slapped her ass cheeks. Dev got bold enough to reach out and start to squeeze first one breast and then the other as he stroked his own cock, getting off to the sight of the other man's cock pounding in and out of the submissive girl's body.

"Careful brother." Loch whispered. "You're drooling. Either mix the drinks or get in the mix and make your mark on her." He was trying hard not to laugh, and Viper couldn't help but smirk back.

"You know if I get into that then no one else is gonna have a turn. I outlast every man in his place."

"Except me." Loch chuckled, popping his jaw as Dagger came to a shuddering finish.

"Yeah you wish, asshat." Viper laughed then slapped both palms down on the bar to get the attention of the members before another one decided to take a turn with Betty. "Hey. Don't break the shiny new toy on night one guys. Come get some shots, give the girl a chance to catch her breath."

All six men left Betty on the floor, where she had sunk to her knees to catch her breath and strolled to the bar. Each was talking about what they intended to do now that they could each make their move on the party favor.

"Fella get those drinks going. This is a party, not just about the hired pussy. We're here to have a damn good time." He was busy mixing and pouring drinks, shots, opening beer, and didn't have time to help Betty to get up but Loch slowly took her to the bathroom for a chance to refresh. He was, mostly, happy that it was his blood brother taking care of her when he couldn't because any of the other members would take advantage of the solitude and not give her the break that she was going to need to get through the night and the rest of the club. He knew, even if she didn't, that she wouldn't be going to bed that night until she had been fucked by every man in the room, including him.

7

"Hey Viper! Focus on the work man before you spill that whiskey and I make you lick it up." Blades said with a smirk. "Wait a minute, that reminds me of something." He looked around the room. "Where is that pretty little piece you brought us? Hand me that box on top of the cooler, there's a little something inside of it that will be perfect for playing with her."

Loch escorted Betty back in from the hall bathroom. "Someone looking for this?"

"Yes I am. Come on over here, darlin'. I have something special for ya." Blades held out the black box as she walked up to him, past the five other men who were smiling hungrily. When she met Viper's eyes, he flashed her a confident grin, she was doing amazing and certainly better than he thought she would have. He was glad that the bar was between them because his cock was straining against his jeans, so hard that he knew if he didn't get involved in the next round of fucking that he was going to have to rub one out behind the bar. If his brother or one of the others caught him doing that, he'd never live it down and would have to explain why he wasn't using the girl he'd brought for that exact purpose.

"A present? Really?" Betty's voice was a song teasing his

already hardened cock.

He'd love to be the one giving her a present, hours and hours in bed together where she would enjoy every second. His very graphic daydream was interrupted by Betty's gasp as she opened the box and lifted out her 'gift'.

"What is it?" Betty asked, Viper watched her lift a shot glass rounded into the gentle bulb of an anal plug. It held about two ounces and to anyone that wasn't familiar with this kind of fun it might look like some cosplayer's potion bottle, but that wasn't the kind of magic if was intended for.

"That is a tasty tail." Viper said, pulling all eyes to him as he started to grab the cream liquors that would be used to fill the glass. "I'll get you lubed up and feed that little baby into you, then position you on the bar, pour shots into that glass and then lick it clean. You have to stay still, or you'll spill the drink."

"What happens if I spill?" She asked, her eyes wide, staring into his.

"If you spill then who ever is licking gets to spank you." Viper said, arching a brow, daring her to squirm or protest. "Bare handed or with a spoon, but I think most of the men here are going to choose to put their hands on that pretty white ass of yours. I want to make it cherry red myself."

Betty blushed as the rumble of men's voices calling for shots began to grow. Ox stepped up to the bar. "Get her ready Viper and then let's get some Irish Cream into her, then we'll add some Bailey's." The men erupted into laughter and Viper grabbed the bottle of lube before taking Betty by the hand and leading her into the kitchen.

"You ever had one of these in you?" He asked, preparing the toy before lathering the lube across her asshole.

"Yeah, I've got some toys from an ex. It's been a while though so take it a little easy, okay?"

"Bend over and spread those cheeks." He was relieved that she wasn't new to this kind of play since she was going to have a terribly busy night. His relief turned to delight when Betty's back arched, and she let a little moan past her lips as he started to push the bulb past her entrance. "Oh Betty. Baby girl I think you like this." He pulled back slightly and nudged it forward again, grinning when Betty grunted her pleasure at the intrusion. He played the plug a little more, his grin growing as she pressed back against the toy.

"Before tonight is over, I am going to put my cock where this toy is and watch you come apart on me." He growled, giving her ass a slap before he slid his hand between her legs. "Oh yes, you like that idea, don't you?" She was dripping wet, juices running down her thighs. "You have no idea how badly I want to stretch you out right now." She bit her lips, moaning softly as he kept playing with her hole. "I wanna pound that soaking wet pussy then finish my load deep between these cheeks. You gonna call my name then Betty?" He reached his second hand to start rubbing her clit with just enough pressure to drive her out of her mind with need but not enough to let her release.

"Oh god. Please Viper? Just a little more?" She whimpered so prettily it hurt his balls.

"Not yet baby but soon. Keep doing what you're doing out there and this weekend will be a lot more fun. They like you, and I think you like them. Just remember to tell me if anyone is too rough or scares you, alright?" He slipped a finger between her folds and pressed his thumb to the bundle of nerves that made her tremble in his grip. "Don't cum yet. Not until I am buried balls deep in you, then I'll make you scream for me."

She nodded, breathlessly close to orgasm, and her knees were shaking but she managed to walk down the hall in her heels.

Viper slid his fingers into his mouth savoring the sweet flavor of her as he listened to the whistles of appreciation as the others all saw the shot glass glistening between her creamy round ass cheeks.

“Alright.” He clapped his hands together. “Let’s get our pretty little toy ready to take those shots guys. What’s up first? Irish Cream?”

Loch stepped up to the bar and smirked at his younger brother. “I think I’ll take that first shot, since I missed out on the fun earlier.”

“Sounds fair to me.” Ox said picking Betty up by her waist. “Bend your knees baby.” He commanded, so that he could set her on the top of the bar and bury his face in her tits, shaking it back and forth until the soft globes were slapping him in the face as he laughed. She presented the pair with an arched back, but it was her hands that everyone, including Viper, was watching.

Betty had been a passive participant in the earlier activities, but now she was responding to Ox as if they were long time lovers. Her fingers were threading through Ox’s long hair, then scratching across his back, leaving marks that crisscrossed bright red while the big man kneaded and bit her breasts with voracious enthusiasm. There wasn’t a limp cock in the room when Betty’s knees slid apart on the marble of the bar top. Every one of them could see the glistening pink of her damp pussy and more than one of them were staring as they unfastened their belts and began to slowly stroke their cocks.

Viper had the creamy alcohol ready, chilling in a bucket of ice that he knew would get a reaction when the icy liquid filled the shot glass that was filling her. She was glorious. No longer playing shy and innocent, Betty was putting on the show he had known she was capable of the day she had auditioned in the strip club. She could have put all those other girls on the stage to shame. She was letting out her wild side now and it was going to be a hell of a show.

8

Betty couldn't believe how good it felt to give in to the desire, the utter and complete lust of the moment. Ox wasn't Viper and neither was Loch, who was watching her with as much amusement in his eyes as there was desire, but they were gorgeous men and they wanted her. They wanted to help her scratch the itch, ease the ache, that was caused by the shot glass toy between her cheeks and the promise from Viper that she would finally feel him inside her, and she was willing to let them help her. It would be even more fun because Viper was watching, his dark eyes shining at her. She knew, and could tell that he knew, when they came together it would be unlike anything else that would happen that night.

Ox was busy devouring her breasts, his mouth and hands exploring every inch of her chest. Instead of feeling exposed and embarrassed Betty put on the show of a lifetime, enjoying every sharp bite that was followed by the wet swipe of a tongue and the rough pad of Ox's thumb across her nipple. Her hand slid from his shoulders to her own thighs. She had been going to slide a pair of her fingers between her lips when she felt a pair of hands on her ankles. At the same time Loch pushed Ox out of the way; not gently either.

"Hello sugar. Ready to play?" He said with a smirk that

made her smile and stop her hands. "I don't want to get my shirt dirty when those knees give out." Her jaw dropped when he peeled the white tank top off to reveal abs that were covered in ink and looked like they were cut out of stone.

"Yeah, I guess we can play. What's the game?" She asked, unable to believe the tremor in her voice.

"It's called 'shot in the ass'. Spin around and plant your forearms on the counter and I'll show you how we play."

The way he looked at her made Betty bite her lip and do as he ordered with an excited smile. If Viper was sexy in a way that made her think of fun and danger, then Loch was pure sin of a sexual nature. She gasped and arched her back when he pressed the topper of the plug forward until it was fully encased between her cheeks. The men were going to be licking alcohol out of a shot glass that was up her ass. None of the anal games she had played had ever been like this, but she had never been put on display as a sex toy before either.

"Fill 'er up, Vipe." Loch said, slapping his hand against her thigh, then running it up to grip a handful of her round ass cheek. "I'm just dyin' of thirst."

She turned her head to meet Viper's eyes, he was almost smiling but with a hint of anger at the man positioned behind her and she knew just how to get to him.

"Don't be mad. The man is thirsty, Viper and I'm ready to be filled."

The men laughed and clapped their hands, eventually making even Viper smile. It was heart-stopping and Betty's jaw dropped just before he winked and picked up a bottle dripping with flakes of ice.

"As the lady says." Viper said, shaking his head with a smirk and raising the bottle over her back.

Ice cold water sprinkled over her back, making her shudder, and making Loch grip her tighter. She couldn't help but wonder if he was going to leave bruises on her hips or, if by the time the weekend was done she would be able to tell what mark on her body came from whom. The cold between her cheeks, where the glass was filling made her want to shiver. She had to stay still though, no spilling.

"Now, now." Loch growled against her cheek, his finger running around the rim of the glass. "Don't move Betty or you'll spill and that would be alcohol abuse. We can't have that, can we?"

She shook her head slowly before laying it on the bar, facing Viper who was running a pair of fingers over the cock straining against the confinement of his jeans. He was watching her as the Loch's large hands took hold of her and his lips danced across her skin before his tongue flicked the edge of the glass. Viper shifted his stance and then Betty could see her reflection in the mirror behind the bar. Loch was poised behind her with a hungry look that made her hold her breath. What was he going to do? How was he going to take the shot?

"Pretty little thing." He murmured then speared his tongue into the creamy liquid filling the cup. She watched his eyes close while his hands kneaded her gently, then one slid down from her ass to begin to tease and circle between her legs. The pressure added to the plug by his tongue, the way it moved as the powerful man licked the cream from between her cheeks was joined by the flick and tease of his fingertip. She wanted more from him, from any of them, in that moment. She needed release; of the pressure, of the building tension, of the pleasure, and she needed it now. Just as she opened her mouth to ask for it Loch swirled his tongue in the glass and flicked his finger against her clit just hard enough to take the edge off her desire.

"That was right tasty. Who's next then? I don't know if our little toy can take too many rounds of that boys. Her knees were shaking, and she was clenching. The woman needs to get off soon or she's not going to have enough fun to come back for the next party you fellas decide to plan without me."

Betty turned her head to look at the men gathered round, she was certain that Viper wouldn't be the one to give her what she wanted, but the rest of them had their cocks bared and ready to try and give her the release that she needed so desperately. Dev stepped towards the bar an eager smile on his face, so did one of the guys who's name she hadn't heard yet. He had shaggy dark hair and flashing brown eyes. Just as the dark-haired man reached towards her, she felt the cold sensation of the shot glass being filled and Viper's rich tenor cut the silence.

"I think I have this situation under control, gentlemen. Let me, and some JD, show you how this is done." He said, running his hand from her shoulder to give a light slap to her ass.

She couldn't believe it. Here? Now? FINALLY? Every nerve she had was on fire at the idea of that gloriously beautiful cock that he had fed her stroking her from the inside, but was that how he would give her the relief she needed or would he use his fingers again? His devilish tongue?

"Viper?" She said his name like a pleading question, everything she wanted to ask him summed up in that single word.

"Don't you worry Betty. Just do what I tell you and you'll

enjoy this. So will the boys. We're gonna give them a little show together, now aren't we?"

His hands were sliding all over her, teasing the excited flesh with a gentility she didn't know he had in him.

"Now Betty baby, I just need to move you forward a little bit."

He slowly moved her, though the shot glass already had freezing cold alcohol in it, some splashed down her the crack of her ass to join and drip with the juice of her sexual excitement. He was going to fuck her, in front of everyone else and she would show them all how good sex could be. When they were done watching her with Viper there wouldn't be a hard cock left in the room. She turned her head back towards him, laying it flat on the bar as he stepped right in front of her.

He still had his ball cap on, along with a zipped up hooded sweatshirt over the white t-shirt she knew was underneath and jeans that were tented by his hard on. He was sexy as hell with all his clothes on but when he reached for the zipper on his hoodie, she knew he wouldn't stay that way for long.

The sweater was placed on the table beside him, followed by the ball cap and then, dear god, the t-shirt came off to reveal ink free abs but his impressively defined upper chest was decorated with tattoos that she wanted to trace her fingers and then her tongue over, tasting every delectable inch of him. Loch walked across her line of sight and she swore that she heard him chuckle but her full awareness was only for the chocolate eyes locked with hers as Viper reached to undo his belt and then his zipper.

He was gloriously erect, a bead of moisture at the tip that was so alluring she didn't realize that she had licked her lips until Blades laughed and then commented.

"Viper, the girl is thirsty. You should give her another drink of that snake of yours before you feed it to her. It's the polite thing to do."

9

Betty blinked. Was he really going to let her taste him again?

"Hold on. Let's make sure she's well taken care of. If we're going to be good hosts." Dagger held a straw to her lips. "Drink that baby girl. Cock tastes better with rum, or so the girls tell me."

She took a long suck of the hard alcohol but before she could swallow the sweet burn Viper had stepped free of his jeans and was pressing the head of his shaft through her lips. The sweaty salt of him with the sweetness of the dark rum was delicious in ways she had never considered.

Viper's fingers stroked across her hair then gripped the base of her high ponytail and thrust slowly, deeply as she swallowed him and the alcohol at the same time. She didn't want him to stop, the feel of him, the smell and the firm pressure of his hands was a heady feeling of surrender that felt incredible to give in to.

Just as she swallowed the last of the rum he pulled out of her mouth, smiling when she whimpered her protest. He stroked her forehead with the pad of his thumb before he stepped out of her line of sight. She could hear and feel him climb onto the bar behind her. It was going to happen, at last. They would put on the sexiest show these guys had ever seen, wild and passionate, hot, and heavy, that would be her first time with Viper. Her lips were spread in a sarcastic, knowing smile, until he spoke again while he poured more cold liquid into the glass, letting it spill across her cheeks.

"Now Betty. I am going to do whatever I want, wherever I want and you, sweetheart, aren't going to move. If that shot glass is empty when I'm done because you spilled it over these sweet cheeks, then I'll have to smack your ass until it's as red as your lips. You don't want to disappoint me, do you Betty baby? You'll be a good girl and do as you're told, won't you?"

"I'll do my best Viper." She managed to say, not sure how she would be able to do what he wanted if he did what he said he was going to. "Ouch!"

"You'll do as your told or I'll do that again." He said, after pinching her hard and almost making her jump. "Let's try that again. You'll do as you're told, won't you Betty?"

"Yes, Viper. I'll do as I'm told." She said, regaining her smile when she saw the amazement on the other men's faces.

"That's my girl." He said, giving her ankle a squeeze.

She turned her head to watch him in the mirror, she didn't want to miss a second of his face and certainly didn't want the others to see her face. Her heart was pounding, and her body was humming as Viper got on the bar top behind her, more naked than she was and still gloriously aroused. If they had been alone, she would have had her hands and her mouth all over him, they would have fought for the dominant role and he would have won, after she enjoyed the fight. Tonight she had to do everything he said, when he said it, but the look in his eyes gave her hope that there would be more and she was determined that, by the end of the weekend, he wouldn't want to share her with anyone because he would want her all to himself.

He was behind her now, his hands caressing her in a way that made her want to close her eyes and relax. She could let him do anything and it would feel good because he was that good. There was no doubt in her mind that he just might be the best she would ever have but this was not the moment that she would find out just how great he could be. That would come later but she would find a way to be alone with him and convince him that they needed to have some privacy, in a bed, with no one to impress but each other.

"No daydreams Betty. You're going to need to focus if you're going to do what I say. Understand? Focus on me and what I'm doing."

"Just on you Viper." Betty nodded, trying to calm her breathing though she had never been more excited.

"I'm going to fuck you and you're going to try not to move. If the glass is empty when I am done, I'll take a belt to these cheeks. If it's not then instead of using our cocks on you, we will all use our mouths instead. I hope you don't disappoint because the boys should really taste that sweet honey of yours."

"Fuck me." Was all she could think to say. How could she stay still with him inside her? He was going to torture her because she wanted him so bad and he knew just how to make her enjoy it.

Slowly he pressed against her, filling inch by inch, stretching with that delicious pleasure that was almost painful it was so intense. If she hadn't gotten so wet from the shots and then sucking on him there was no way she could have taken him in without it hurting. He was the biggest man she had ever had, and she wouldn't be able to deny it because even though she was dripping wet he was having a hard time fitting himself inside her.

"Either Betty is as tight as a nun's snatch or she's never had a real magnum size dick in her before." Loch said with a laugh, taking Viper's spot behind the bar and standing just barely inside her line of sight so he didn't block her view of the man slowly working his cock between her legs. If it had been anyone else, she didn't think that she would notice the fact that his jeans were undone and that he was slowly stroking himself in rhythm with his brother. Did they ever share women? They didn't seem to like each other much, but she caught a few shared glances in the mirror that ended with both of them looking at her. The idea of being between them both, without the others watching sent a fresh wave of heated arousal between her legs and Viper nudged in a little further.

"That's it, baby. Let me in like a good girl and this will feel really good."

His words were an aphrodisiac and her mouth dropped open as he sank home the last few inches, sheathing himself completely with a deep groan. His hands gripped her cheeks hard enough to leave marks and she fought to be still as he withdrew and slid firmly back again. It was agony, excruciatingly slow and completely blissful. She had no control except to be as still as she could, to keep the cold alcohol in the glass so that she could get the reward rather than the belt that she knew would sting but not hurt, this was all part of the game that she was determined to win. With the man attached to the amazing cock that was filling her as the prize she was going to win.

"Look how good the girl is Viper. Almost completely still. If it weren't for those breathy little moans and the way her toes are curling, I'd think you were fucking a real toy instead of our pretty little thing." Blades said with a laugh when he set his hand on Betty's hair, stroking the ponytail and watching her face as Viper increased his speed. He did not make a comment about Loch enjoying the show, so she guessed that the rest of them were too.

"Turn your head for me sweetheart." He said gently using her pony-tail to turn her head from Loch and the mirror to face the room of men who were all watching her body shake as the thick shaft stroking her from the inside out edged her closer to the release she needed.

"You should show some appreciation for your audience dear. These boys aren't stroking off to Viper. You're the one they want to see and you're the one they will see."

It was as if he knew that she was getting close. She wanted to close her eyes and feel every single stroke that was sending her over the edge, but this was about the show and not about her. Viper's thumb rubbed a circle on her ass cheek, and she felt a shift in his hips. He stroked across her g-spot and thoughts of everything else stopped. Her body wanted to buck back against him, to give him as much as he was giving to her, but she couldn't. He was holding her so tight that the only way that drink was going to spill is if he spilled it, or if he let go of her.

Her jaw fell open as she let loose the moan of pleasure that was building. Her eyes closed and she felt like she was going to explode from the inside out.

“Oh my god…Viper!” She cried out, her hands clawing at the counter in frustration and ecstasy at the same time. She barely heard the round of applause from the club members, but she felt the surge as the man behind her emptied himself inside her then bent down to suck the shot glass empty.

10

"Good girl, Betty." Blades said, patting her cheek as Viper withdrew with a hand caressing down her leg. She was amazing and more than ever Viper knew he wanted to have her alone, no one watching, to see what wildness she was capable of.

He stepped down from the bar and pulled his jeans back on, leaving his shirt off so she could see his tattoos. In comparison to the other members he and his brother were the most inked and he had noticed the slight dilation in her pupils at the sight so there was no doubt that she liked it.

"Pretty good show, Viper." Ox said, running his fingers through his long hair. "Can't wait to see if I get a better reaction when it's my turn."

Resting his hand on Betty's calf he looked over his shoulder at Loch and they shared a nod of understanding, they would both do whatever they could to delay that happening. They might fight over most things, but once they decided to join forces, they were undefeated. If Ox thought he was going to get Betty to himself, to fuck or whatever he was wanting to do. Only the brothers would get that special privilege and they'd do it under the guise of being her caretakers for the weekend. Viper didn't relish the idea of sharing her with anyone , but there was no option for now and if he had to share, he could trust that Loch wouldn't try to keep her, he never kept anyone.

"Well I think that our little Betty might need a break after that. The poor girl still has shaking knees." Viper said, circling his thumb on her ankle. "I'll get her fed and a little rest before any more socializing with you lot." He chuckled at the protests and faked indignation before helping Betty down from the bar. "Just give us a few minutes. Loch can mix the drinks for a few minutes."

He led the way towards the kitchen, forcing his hands not to clench when he heard the sound of hands slapping flesh. The only way he was going to get through this weekend was to do the opposite of his plan, which had been to avoid fucking her until the last day so that she could see that their chemistry was incredible. For now he was going to have to show the others that it didn't matter what they did or how many times she sat on their cocks or their faces, like Dev was currently telling the others he intended to spend some time doing, she was going to be his.

He was far from Romeo or the billionaire playboys with yachts and spank closets that filled the books that the girls the other men brought around talked about while he tended the bar. He was going to try to be something even more impressive: a decent man.

“Let me take that thing out of you.” He said, bending her over one of the padded kitchen stools. “Then you can have something to eat and rest a bit. They’ll get drunk and rowdy for a bit, bragging about anything they can think of and then, when they’re a little bit mellow, I’ll bring you back out. We can save the wild stuff for tomorrow night. There will be a few more members here, not all of them are into public displays so they might not take you up on your talents or might want private time.”

“Private time? One on one in a room?” She asked, sounding nervous as she got a glass and water from the tap. “Is it safe? Are they safe?”

He laughed, setting the glass plug in the dishwasher, and standing to face her.

“Baby girl, not one man here could ever be called ‘safe’. I don’t have time to tell you the things we do when we’re not here and I really don’t think you want to know. The thing that I can tell you is that you are safe here. Not one of us would hurt you, unless you wanted it for fun, but I don’t think that is your kink.”

Her eyes twinkled back at him before he opened the fridge and dug out some plates from the earlier meal where she had been the centerpiece.

"Eat anything you want and drink lots of water. You're going to need to be hydrated for the rest of the fun in store for you."

He watched while she piled a plate with meat and vegetables. Chuckling when she stared at the potatoes then sat down without touching them.

"You want 'em? Just eat. Not one person in this place is gonna judge you. Except me." He winked, which got him the blush he wanted as he grabbed a handful of cherries to eat while she dined.

"You're judging me? On what? Sexual performance? If so, telling me that I'm not allowed to move isn't fair." She protested, licking her lips casually. She couldn't have known that it made any man watching her wonder what else she might do with that tongue and what those lips would feel like on their body. Or did she know? She was watching him expectantly. Fuck, she had asked him a question.

"What am I judging? You for not even trying those potatoes just because you think you're not skinny enough, or something like that." He shrugged and spit the pits into a bowl. "They're good. You should eat them, you're beautiful and you want them." He slid the bowl across the counter towards her. “C’mon. I won’t tell and then the calories don’t count. Isn’t that how it works.”

“Wow.” She said with a shocked smile and shook her head.

“What? Can’t believe I’m not a complete monster?” He said, leaning towards her.

“No. I can’t believe you think I’m not eating them because I care what you think.” She grabbed a handful of the potatoes and tossed them at him. “They’re heavy and I intend to dance.” She retorted with a laugh.

She was staring at him, on the verge of bursting into laughter as he brushed the potatoes off his shoulder, a small piece fell from the brim of his hat which sent her over the edge. If anyone else had done that he might have been annoyed, even pissed off but she was so giddy, innocent, and genuine, he couldn't help the grin he felt spreading across his face. "Oh, you think that's funny, do you?" He asked, coming around the edge of the kitchen island and stalking towards her.

“I think it’s damn hilarious.” She retorted, backing away slowly. “The big man with potato on his face.”

“Come here and I’ll show you what we do to food wasters around here Missy.”

He ran at her and she bolted to the other side of the island, her laugh echoing around the room as he chased her. With the heels on she couldn't run too fast and so it was only a few laps around the island before he locked his arms around her waist and growled in her ear.

"Gotcha. What'll you do now baby?"

She squirmed and struggled in his arms. It made him laugh that she thought she could get away if he didn't want her to. He spun her around to face him and pinned her lower body to the counter with the press of his hips. His hands on either side of her, Viper knew that he had her trapped and the way she pressed back against him said she didn't mind the restraint.

"The bigger, and I do mean bigger, question, is what are you going to do next Viper?"

She purred his name while one hand slid between them to cup his package through his jeans and the other traced the edge of his ear and down his neck. He was aroused, and with her eyes daring him to make a move, he made a snap decision.

"I'm going to teach you a lesson you're never going to forget."

He wrapped a hand into her hair and pulled her close for a kiss that was anything but gentle. Hard and punishing with every press of his lips and sweep of his tongue he wanted her to know that he could own her in ways that no man that she had ever been with could have done. He could take her: mind, body and soul, there would be no protest and no going back, not tonight and not Sunday when she left this place. The only question wasn't if she wanted him, it wasn't even: did he want her? but was he really ready for this or would it destroy the party and get him booted from the program?

11

She was just as in the moment as he was, he loved how her fingertips were dancing across his skin. They might leave marks, but he didn't care. There was something in him that needed to push her to the limit of her passion and him to the edge of his control. He needed to see her come undone by his touch. He wanted to see if the wildness he thought he had seen in her eyes was really a part of her or just something that had been brought out by the heat of the moment.

The hand that wasn’t in her hair, keeping her lips connected to his, was kneading her breast. The soft flesh plumped in his hand, heavy with her arousal as she moaned against his teeth. She wanted him as badly as he wanted her and, damn him to hell, he couldn’t think of a reason to hold back. When her clever little fingers unfastened his belt and the fly of his jeans Viper smiled, broke the kiss, and bit the sensitive trigger point on her neck.

It must have driven her wild because her hand was inside his pants, pulling him free as she hopped up onto the counter. Wrapping her legs around his waist, Betty pulled him close and whispered those two words he was dying to hear from her.

“Fuck me.”

"As the lady asks." He chuckled and pulled her towards him. This would be as fast as it would be intense, then time to take her back upstairs to rest before going back to the party. He could feel the heat from her core, one more inch forward and he would be able to spear her with a single hard thrust.

"Ready baby girl?" He growled against her rapidly beating pulse, dragging his teeth across her collarbone when he felt a drip of her moisture on the tip of his cock. "Because I am going rock your fucking world."

"Sorry man but world rocking will have to wait." Loch said from the doorway. "Unless you want some help to get her going faster." He added with a smirk that told Viper that his older brother knew exactly what was going on.

"Get bent." Viper snapped back, holding off on his penetration until he knew what was going on. He had no intention of starting something he couldn't finish properly. "I have no time to wait for you to get it up enough to be of any use this time."

Betty's eyes flew open wide in surprise. She must have guessed that he and his brother had shared girls over the years. Sometimes it was just the same girl and sometimes it was the same bed at the same time. If she hadn't guessed it before she was thinking about it now. Her breath was quicker, and he could see the increase in her pulse, smell her excitement and he wondered if she wanted that, to be shared between him and his brother?

"Little brother, I am already there." Loch replied with a laugh as he stepped up to the counter and took Betty's head out of his hand to kiss her with a lazy, penetrating sweep of his tongue.

She shifted her hips to turn into the kiss and that little shift moved her just enough to take the tip of Viper's shaft into her dripping wet pussy. A flick of their eyes and a mutual understanding passed between him and his older brother. This might not be the claiming that he had been intending but it would certainly elicit the response he was hoping for in her. If he had to share for a time, he would rather it be Loch than Ox. Girls fell in love with the long-haired mountain of a man, but he never saw that until he had already broken their hearts.

Betty gasped, breaking the kiss with his brother when he adjusted to sink home between her thighs, and everything escalated from there in a whirlwind. Loch kept his mouth and a hand on Betty while the other pushed the food and dishes aside so that they could lay her across the cold marble to enjoy her completely with ease.

As soon as her back was on the marble Viper increased the motion of his hips, stroking her from the inside as his brother devoured as much of her body as possible. Leaning from across the island to suckle her nipples until she was squirming and bucking against the cock buried in her. It was hard to hold her still but from the way the sweat was dewing on her skin he knew that she was enjoying every second of this game.

While his hand gripped her hips, on the other side of the counter Loch was unzipping his own fly to feed Betty his shaft that was, as he said, already there. Watching her take a cock in her mouth while his own pounded her from the other end was hotter than he expected and when she moaned and clenched around him, he grinned in response. In sync with the other's thought both brothers reached to caress her breasts, teasing each nipple until it was beaded, and Betty's back was arching with her need.

Seeing her spread out in front of him, writhing and bucking to his rhythm Viper knew he wasn't going to last much longer, and Loch's face had the same look and so he grunted to his brother. "Flip?"

"Flip." Was the terse reply.

Both pulled out of their respective pleasure holes and grabbed the girl by the hips and shoulders to flip her onto her stomach to make the final moments before release, easier for all three of them. He thundered into her and Loch threaded his fingers behind her head to hold her just as he wanted while he fucked her mouth.

"Holy fuck, Betty." Viper growled, emptying himself into her then giving her ass a slap as he pulled out and watched Loch increase his speed so he could finish down the hot vacuum of her throat. He watched as her eyes closed first and then so did his, the grunt of satisfaction a sure tell that he had shot a load between those cherry red lips. Now that they had shared her once it was sure to happen again. It was possible that his brother would even help keep Betty from spending too much time alone with Ox. They had grown up sharing everything, and always having the other's back as a united front, it wasn't about to change now.

"Well, that wasn't what I came in here for, but it was sure worth the trip." Loch laughed and reached for a beer from the fridge, handing one to Betty and then tossing one back to Viper.

"Obviously not." Viper grinned and eased Betty up from the counter so she could enjoy the drink. "So, what was it that was so important that you had to disturb us?"

He took a long swig from the bottle in his hand, then pointed the long neck towards the door. "They wanted to know how long of a rest Miss Betty was going to need. Every one of them is eager for her company it would seem. Not that I blame them."

“I can go back out there now.” Betty said with a smile. She hopped off the counter and almost fell over.

Loch reached for her, but it was Viper that caught her, holding her close to his chest so the sweetness of her scent filled his nostrils.

“I don’t think you’re quite ready for that yet. Why not take a bit of rest, alone, upstairs? One of us will come to get you in an hour so you’re rested for the rest of the night.” Viper said, his thumbs making circles on her arms.

“Trust me, you’re gonna need that with how popular you are with that crowd, young lady.” Loch added with an arched brow when he noticed Viper’s hands.

“I’m surprised that there aren’t more people here.” Betty said, leaning her head against Viper with a tired expression. The intensity of the evening was catching up with her and she didn’t even know it yet.

“Well, to come to these parties there are certain rules for us, like there was for you.” Viper said, guiding her towards the stairwell with Loch right behind him.

“Does that mean you guys are all on birth control too?” She asked sleepily.

“Something like that.” Viper laughed and gave her ass a friendly swat.

"Hey, I got snipped years ago." Loch quipped from behind them both.

He was obviously going to follow them upstairs to make sure that Betty got to rest, and that Viper didn't join her in the bed for another round.

"That's the best news I've had this week." Viper retorted back. "No need to worry about you pro-creating. The last thing we need is your spawn running amuck all over the world."

"Well we can agree on that at least. You've probably got a few little rug rats out there somewhere."

Betty giggled at the banter. "So, Loch doesn't need a pill, but what about the rest of you? You said there were rules? That means there are others who aren't here yet?"

"The ones who aren't here yet won't be here this weekend." Viper said, opening the door to her room. "It means they didn't pass a blood test to let them go bareback without a risk to you or let's just say, you wouldn't have been safe if some other members were here."

Loch nodded and looked around the room at the costumes and shoes.

"He's right. If you think guys like Ox or Dagger are intimidating a few of the other guys make them look like teddy bears. If you come out a second time you might meet them, they're not allowed to play with rookies like you."

"I'm a rookie?" She asked, stretching as she sat on the bed.

The arch of her back sent a familiar twitch to Viper's cock but she really did need the rest.

"You're a rookie alright. If you weren't, you'd know that doing that is practically inviting either of us to join you in that bed. As much fun as it would be, you are supposed to be resting because you won't see it again until close to three in the morning. Take advantage of it because there's a hungry crowd waiting for your return."

The brothers both left the room when she was under the covers, locking the door from the inside before closing it behind them.

"You're a damned idiot." Loch said when they were back in the kitchen.

"What do you mean?" Viper asked, taking his beer back from the counter before he looked out the window at the arriving vehicles. "Support crew is here to clean up in here so say what you want to say before they get in here or keep it to yourself."

"You like her. You brought a girl you like to be fucked by the club for the weekend and think I'm not going to see it?"

Loch opened the fridge for another bottle and shook his head before downing half of it. "You're either naive as fuck or just plain stupid. Which is it?"

"I'm neither, and you're an ass by the way. That's why I didn't invite you." Viper growled and finished his drink. Right or wrong he didn't need to be reminded by his older brother how stupid it was to develop feelings for a girl that was meant to be passed around to every man in this place and more if she came back again.

"I just met her yesterday. The girl is cute and fun, what's not to like about her." He shrugged and tossed the bottle. Crossing his arms across his chest his glare challenged the other man to prove that it was more than a casual attraction.

"Oh, I don't know, the fact that me and six of your badge brothers are going to spend the next two days screwing every hold she has while you watch and join." Loch set his own empty bottle down and stalked towards Viper. "And you'll join baby brother or else every man out there is going to think what I'm thinking. If they think they see it then they will be merciless until they get you to admit it. Do you want that for her?"

He jerked his head towards the door, glaring at Loch. "She knows what she signed on for so don't act like I brought a nun or kid here. She is a full-grown woman and in case you didn't notice she is having a great time. I did that for her."

He straightened from the counter and uncrossed his arms before turning towards the doors to the main room.

"And as for the sharing, I've shared girls with you and dated them for months. You might not be able to play nice with others, but as long as I know where her heart is and what bed she wants to be in at the end of the day, I can play all day."

12

It was almost an hour later, and Viper couldn't stop checking his watch to see if it was time to go wake Betty up. He had laughed and joked with Ox and the others, avoiding Loch as much as he could. Every so often he would feel eyes on him and look up to see his brother watching him, that smug, knowing look in his eyes. It made Viper want to throw down and go bare knuckles fighting against him until he said that he was wrong about Betty, that he had been talking out of his ass the whole time. It would never happen though because he was right about almost all of it.

"Eager to go wake up our little plaything Viper?" Blades said, distracting him from glaring again by gripping his shoulder. "I think it's about time she made another appearance, don't you?"

"Sure thing, Blades." He said, slamming back the bourbon in his glass and tipping his ball cap to the senior member. "I'll go get her ready and bring her down."

"Nothing too fancy this time, boy." Dagger called from the bar.

There weren't too many members in his club that would call him 'boy' like that, not with his record, but Dagger was one of them. He was also right on the edge of the safe members that he had warned Betty about earlier. If he weren't second in command of the club there was no way he would have been allowed even though he swore he would be on his best behavior since Betty was new to this scene.

"You got it. Nice and simple." He said, heading towards the kitchen doors. Taking the steps two at a time he was surprised when he reached the top and found a light on in the room.

"Betty? It's Viper. Can you open the door for me?" He asked, tapping his knuckles on the door. "Time to go downstairs."

She opened the door with a bright smile, completely naked. His jaw dropped in surprise.

"Well hello there. That's a hell of a way to answer the door Betty. What if I had Loch or Ox with me?" He said, stepping inside and closing the door behind him.

"You would have said so, or I would have heard them when you thundered up the stairs." She retorted cheekily, crossing her arms, and pushing her already perky breasts higher.

He wanted to take each one in his mouth and suck on them until she was aching with need that he would deny her like he had to deny himself, for now at least.

"Well if I don't hurry up and get you back down there then at least one of them will come up those stairs looking for both of us and I'd rather you were at least getting ready instead of standing here naked and looking so damned fuckable my balls hurt."

"Aww do I hurt your balls Viper?" She asked coyly with a tilt of her head.

"Why don't you just get dressed so we can go back downstairs." He tossed her a mini-skirt and tube top with a grin. "Mine aren't the only balls aching because of you, Missy. As much as I would enjoy a little one-on-one if I don't get you back to the party it won't be my balls that hurt. Everyone is waiting and I am supposed to be behind the bar in a few minutes."

She pulled on the clothes and a pair of knee-high boots that resembled combat boots, but she was hotter than any soldier he'd ever seen before.

"Alright. Ready to go and have a party. I look okay?" She asked with a smile that sent a jolt to his heart.

He had to stop thinking like that, at least until Sunday night when he drove her home.

"Yeah babe, you look great. Add that cherry lipstick from before and it'll be perfect." He opened the door. "Let's have a party."

Her appearance through the swinging kitchen door was greeted by a few cheers and a round of raised beer from the men standing at the bar.

"Looks like the party is back boys, and in boots this time. Looking good Betty." Ox said, clapping his hands eagerly as Betty sauntered over to him, accepting the beer he cracked open for her.

Viper took his spot behind the bar, taking the bottle opener from Dev and grabbing the bottle of bourbon to pour himself a double while the members, some drunker than others, started to chat up Betty. Their hands were all over her and Blades even pulled her into his lap, his hand between her legs as they all talked.

He smirked when his eyes met Loch who was just waiting to see him lose his cool. It wasn't going to happen and if that idiot was going to watch him all night then he was going to have some fun proving 'big brother' wrong.

"Hey boys why don't we set up some fun for our little party favor?" He started to mix a tray of shots and grabbed a few bottles of whipped cream from the cooler.

"Muff dives and titty shots anyone?" He called, slamming back his own shot before shaking the cream.

"You gonna be able to mix them if you keep drinking like that?" Rex asked. He and Doc had been silent participants for most of the night, they weren't big talkers, but of course Rex had to pick now to speak up. "Yeah, I'll be fine, thanks Rex. Unless the only cream you wanna get is in a shot glass you'll shut your pie hole."

The other man held up his hands but every other man in the room was looking at Viper and the bottle beside him.

"Hey, have I ever made mistakes on your drinks before there was a hot chick in the room? No? Then I'm not going to do it now."

He gave Blades a nod "Why don't we help our guest get a little more comfortable for this? After all, it's all about her, not me."

"How about the dinner table." Doc suggested. "Since she looks about good enough to eat."

"I think you're right Doc." Loch agreed, walking up to Betty, and taking her mouth in a long, lazy kiss. "Definitely needs to be served up just right."

He led her to the table while Viper prepared the creamy shot that would be served in the bowl of whipped cream that would be placed over her pussy and the drinker would find the glass with his tongue and lips before downing it.

Something similar would be done between her breasts and if the way that everyone else was acting was any indication he knew that he would need to make sure that there were enough shots for everyone to have a go before things escalated into the fuckery that he knew was coming.

She looked so sexy laying in the middle of the dining table. Her hair was spread out around her and her back was arched just enough that it didn't touch the table. Her feet were resting on the table for now but once he started to serve the shots, they would be hanging off the edge to give the man taking the shot the best access to the whipped cream.

Blades and Dagger didn't seem to be interested in the shots. They looked satisfied to sit and watch everyone having a good time. Viper figured that it wouldn't be too long until the two older men retired for the night, leaving the wilder hours to the younger men. It would be a blur of alcohol and sex until either Betty was too worn out for more fun or the other members got too drunk to get it up.

"Come on man. I'm thirsty." Doc called from the foot of the table, his hands running up and down Betty's calves. "Let's get started."

"Absolutely." Viper replied, bringing the tray of shots and the cans of whipped cream to put on the table. "Let's just get her a little more decorated for the fun, eh?" He started to shake one of the cans, intending to make a whipped cream bikini.

"Save it for later. I want that muff dive right now."

Viper chuckled at the impatient tone. He wondered what kind of jealousy the others would show if they knew that he and Loch had already shared their own private round with her before any of the rest of them? The thought of her cumming around him, losing complete control of herself before crashing over the edge of bliss, screaming his name with each wave of pleasure that he would give her. Over and over he would make her shatter until she was delirious with satisfaction.

He set the bowl with the shot and foamy whip to rest over the crotch of her panties and rested his hand above the bowl while looking down into her eyes.

"Don't move now. As much as we want to make a mess of you, let's take a little time to get there." He winked at her and started to fill up the next bowl.

"While Doc tries to find the prize in all that cream who's ready to bury their face between these, exceptionally beautiful, unbelievably soft, tits to find another shot? What about an extra special kiss?"

He put one of the shot glasses between her breasts, taking

the time to kiss each nipple, swirling his tongue around the bud through the thin fabric of her bra, putting a steadying hand to her stomach when she started to move against him.

"Now, now. Just stay still. Be a good girl, Hun, and you'll get something special by the end of this."

She stuck out her lip, pouting silently at him which made Viper laugh. Lowering his mouth to her he kissed her firmly and when she opened her mouth for more, he slid a shot glass between her teeth and chuckled.

"Always so eager to be a good girl for me, for us, aren't you Betty?" He said with a grin, clapping his hands for the others to enjoy what he'd set up for them. "There you go guys. You couldn't ask for a sweeter setup for fun, could you?"

Ox stepped up to the table so that he could kiss her, his tongue lapping up the drink from between her teeth before sucking the glass into his mouth and tossing his head back to swallow the alcohol before kissing her again. He was devouring her mouth and running his fingers through her hair while he did it.

Dev and Rex were on either side of the table, each of the tracing a fingertip around her nipples while she squirmed. He was fairly sure that the attention of four men was almost too much for her. Her skin was flushed and her eyes blinking rapidly told him that she was completely aroused and fighting her body's reaction. It was amazing to watch her fight her own body and when Loch stood next to him, he couldn't help but comment.

"You think she'll hold it off or do you think she'll have to let it go?"

"Oh, I think she wants to make you proud." Loch said, taking a hit of his drink. "She's going to hold on until you give her a sign she can let go."

The brothers shared a look before the older one said.

"Make her wait, see how much she can take."

13

Every nerve she had was on fire. It was like Viper and his friends were determined to drive her out of her mind so that all she could think about was them and the need to be filled by them, any of them, all of them, she just needed more. With the teasing touch to her breasts and Ox's passionately hungry kiss she was torturously close to the edge, but they kept her just far enough from release to drive her crazy.

The man between her legs, Doc she was sure she had heard someone call him, had found, and finished the shot buried in the bowl. She felt him lift it off her hips, but he didn't move from his position. His breath was hot against her core and if Ox hadn't had his tongue down her throat, she would have begged for a moment to catch her breath. Instead she got a wave of pleasure as his hot, wet, tongue stroked against her.

This was why she hadn't been given panties to go with her skirt. They would have gotten in the way of the fun that they were having with her. She would have wanted to rip them off so that she could have what she had now: a man dining between her thighs, eating her out like it was the last meal he would ever have and that she was the last woman he might ever get to be with. Doc was licking, sucking, and nipping at her while the other three men were making sure that this was a total body experience for her in ways she had never imagined.

Her back arched and she cried out into Ox's mouth. "More! Please? More!"

The big, bearded, man broke their kiss just long enough to say to the man eating her so expertly she was losing her mind. "Someone give the lady what she's asking for and fuck her already."

Doc stood and she could hear him unfasten his belt before he tugged her by her knees to the edge of the table. The trio of other men moved with her, Ox undoing his fly at the same time.

"Let's make this special, shall we?" He said, tugging her mouth open with a smile. "You look like you need a little bit more than Doc can give you. Is that true?"

She nodded, staring up at him with gratitude that he was able to see that she wanted so much more, needed more.

"Yes. Ox? I'm so hungry for more. Help a girl out?" She asked with a smile.

The brothers were watching ravenously, but they didn't move to join the fun or to help ease the growing pressure that was building. They had to know she was in agony and they certainly knew that they had the skills to make sure that she was well satisfied and yet they were simply watching two other men fuck her while another one caressed her breasts. If they wouldn't fuck her then she would make sure that they were out of their minds with regret and lust.

With a single hard thrust Doc was balls deep inside her and he went right to work. His body pumping in and out of hers while Ox fit his giant cock into her mouth. He was more careful this time than he had been when she was on her knees greeting everyone, but it was still a difficult stretch and Betty knew that her jaw was going to ache when he was done. The rest of her was going to feel so good that the future ache really wouldn't matter.

The feeling of Ox's big hands on her head, his fingers threading into her hair, as Doc's gripped her hips to piston himself even faster was beginning to overthrow her senses. When Doc came with a final surge she gagged and swallowed another thick, swollen inch from Ox, just as the man working her chest dragged his teeth across her nipple. She screamed around the shaft in her mouth and her body bucked, writhing with pleasure. Her mind went blank of all thoughts except the euphoria washing over her in wave after blissful wave.

Her eyes were closed, savoring the lingering sensations between her legs while Ox began to increase his pace and she had to concentrate on keeping her jaw relaxed so he could enjoy her. Betty found herself enjoying the choking size of the big man, nudging down her throat a little farther with each press of his hips. Between his cock and the hands that hadn't stopped playing with her nipples she thought she just might cum again then everything shifted.

Blinking rapidly, she looked down her body when she felt a hand spread across her pelvis, pressing her down to hold her squirming hips still; it was Viper.

"Didn't I tell you I'd hold you down. Be a good girl and I'll give you something special."

She tried to nod but Ox's hands made it impossible. He increased his pace, distracting her from the strong hand holding her hips down. She felt Viper's thumb nudge through her damp folds to rub her clit, slowly at first, but then he began to increase his speed. There was one blinding moment of panic when she thought she might choke on Ox but that disappeared the moment Viper slid a finger inside her and began to work the magic that he had given her upstairs and at the strip club.

The four other men began to cheer Viper on, encouraging him to bring her to an orgasm before Ox finished in her throat. She didn't have the strength to open her eyes, but she could hear them as her body began to tremble. It didn't matter which one of the men finished first because she was going to go before either of them if they kept this up.

It was amazing, she was so close, she could feel a blush spread across her body. The men must have been paying attention because she heard one of them comment.

"I don't think she is going to last another ten strokes from Viper."

"Turn her on her side and I'll make sure she goes off like a rocket." Loch said, stepping closer.

Rex and Viper rolled her onto her left side, Ox was too close to release to do anything except thrust his cock down her throat. She could feel Loch behind her, the heat radiating off his bare chest was hard to ignore. He stroked a line down her back with either his finger or knuckle. It wasn't big enough to be his dick. When he paused his touch at the crease of her ass Betty shivered, he wouldn't, would he?

"You boys wanna make a woman cum like never before you gotta give her a little more attention." He said, confidence dripping from his voice. He removed his hand from her backside just as Ox started to twitch in her mouth. He was ready to shoot his load and his entire body was stiffening.

Just when she thought the moment couldn't get any hotter, Viper playing with her g-spot as Rex rolled her nipples into tight buds while Ox shot his burning hot load into her mouth, Loch touched a now wet finger to her asshole and pressed it inside. The sensation of being completely filled, stimulated, and utterly fucked was too much, just enough and everything she didn't know that she had been missing.

She screamed her orgasm around Ox's slowly softening cock. The double finger penetration by the devilish brothers was, by far, the most exquisitely sinful thing she had ever experienced. The rippling waves of ecstasy kept cascading over her senses as Viper, Loch and Rex kept working her body. The roars of apprcciation from the others finally cut through to her awareness and she realized that she must be putting on quite the show as she came again and again.

The men stopped their stimulating play and Betty sat up. The world was a spinning just a little, but her body was humming with satisfaction. The only thing that would have made that better would have been if the brothers were using their cock's instead of their fingers, and the way they were both looking at her said that she just might get that wish granted if she played her cards right.

Both men helped her to her feet and then Viper headed behind the bar to grab her a drink. She felt like a princess with the attention being poured on her from the men as she walked to sit by the bar, between Blades and Dagger. Instead of treating her like a party toy or, an even bigger fear, like a whore, they were treating her like a lady that they adored. Loch even draped his black button up shirt over her shoulders.

“Don’t need you catching a chill. If you’re going to shiver and shake, I’d rather it be due to me blowing that pretty little mind of yours.” He said, tapping her on the nose playfully.

“Well I’d like to see that…or feel that I should say.” Betty retorted with a nip towards his finger before she took the glass held out to her by Viper.

“Double rum and coke. That’s your drink, right?” He said with a nod towards the drink. “You had that the other night at the club.” She took a sip and smiled at him, which brought a smile to his lips that sent a race through her heart.

"Thanks Viper. It's just what I needed after all that." She said, returning the smile her thanks earned her.

"After 'all that' eh?" Loch said with a grin while the others chuckled into their drinks. "And did you like all that fun? I don't think we have asked you what you think of our little party."

Suddenly they were all quiet, staring at her expectantly. She looked over her shoulder at Viper who was polishing a glass, then back to the men around her.

"I'm having more fun than I expected. The way Viper described you all I was expecting big scary bad guys. You're all so nice though "

Ox laughed and gave her a pat on the knee. "We're not really that nice, but I'm glad you think so. It wouldn't be half as fun if you were scared."

"Oh, I don't know." Dagger said beside her. His voice was so low it was practically a growl. He rested his hand on her arm and Betty got chills. It was not hard to believe Viper's words of warning about the senior member being more dangerous than he was acting.

Taking a deep breath, she looked into the eyes of the other men. Ox was right. Behind the laughter and lust these were dark, deadly men.

"There's something about a fearful, uncertain woman that makes me excited." Dagger concluded, winking at Betty before returning his attention to his own drink.

Betty shivered, taking a swig of the cold drink in her hand so that she could blame the reaction on the ice instead of the man beside her. If it had been him and not Viper that had interviewed her for the party, she was certain that she would never had agreed to come here and let them have their fun. The thrilled glint in his eyes when he talked about a scared girl was more terrifying than she wanted to admit.

A finger stroked down her back making her turn around to see Viper leaning over the counter with a concerned look on his face. His eyes flicked to Dagger, who was focused on a story that Doc was telling, everything in the man behind the bar's face was worry for her.

"You okay?" He whispered softly, his fingers gently touching her arm and giving more reassurance than she thought was possible in such a simple gesture.

"Yeah. I'll be alright. I'm glad it was you and not him that auditioned me." She whispered back, sliding her empty glass back towards him. "Could I have another one? Please?"

"As the lady wishes." Viper said, mixing another round for her, looking over her head to someone behind her while he popped the ice cubes from the tray.

Taking her glass back she turned to try and see who he was looking at and found Loch with his eyes locked on her. He gave a nod, whether to her or Viper she didn't know, but he stepped towards her and lifted her off the stool to take her seat and place her on his lap. She felt surprisingly safe in the tattooed arms of Viper's older brother, kind of like a sexy teddy bear. When his chin rested on her shoulder, she relaxed into him instinctively with a soft sigh. He wouldn't let any of

Dagger's twisted fantasies, whatever they might be, happen to her.

"Don't go hogging all those curves Loch." Dev said, stepping up to pull her out of the warmth and relative safety of the big man's lap. "I think the lady needs to dance. Viper, crank up that two-step would ya?"

She watched him chuckle and shake his head, but Viper cranked up a song by some guy that sounded like he was from Louisiana and Dev pulled her onto the floor to dance, pulling her close and resting a hand on her ass while they moved together.

Betty had never danced nearly naked before, but after Dev, she danced with Rex and Doc before Blades nodded to Viper to change the music and took her hand. He pulled her close in a slow R&B dance that was almost like sex on the dance floor. Slowly, carefully, he peeled the bra straps from her shoulders and unfastened the back. He tossed it towards the bar and began to peel her skirt off her hips and down her legs until she was dancing naked with him.

When the song ended Blades kissed her, he tasted like whiskey and a sweet cigar, then ran his hand down her spine to cup her backside.

"If I'd had a few less shots I'd be taking you upstairs

tonight, instead I'll leave you down here with the boys who WILL take good care of you and tuck you into bed so that you're all happy and pretty come coffee time tomorrow morning." He said, giving her a spank between the legs before nodding for Dagger to join him upstairs for whatever they were going to do that didn't include her.

Once they were gone Rex, Doc, and Dev were soon to follow which left Betty alone with the trio of Loch, Viper and Ox. They were all at the bar and so she decided to join them, letting her breasts lay on the cool marble top so that all three of them could stare while she enjoyed her drink.

"What happens now? It's just the four of us." Betty asked, not sure if she was nervous or excited. With the other five members gone it was less like a party and much more intimate, which meant that anything could happen. Anything at all. The trio shared a glance between each other then Loch's hand slid around her waist while Ox teased his fingers through her hair.

"Well, you could keep dancing." Viper suggested, sliding her glass back across the counter to her. "I gotta say I was enjoying the view and I wouldn't mind a turn around the floor myself."

"I'm not a stripper." Betty said, looking towards the stage that had a shiny metal pole on in. "I mean, I could try but I don't think it would be anything other than funny if I did."

"I don't know about these two knuckleheads, but I very rarely find a naked woman funny unless she's trying to be funny." Viper said with a smile, stepping around the bar to hold out a hand to her. "And you can't strip if you're already naked, but we can still dance."

They danced to a song that Betty couldn't quite hear until Viper began to sing softly in her ear while his hand caressed her back and eventually rested on the curve of her ass while they moved together.

She might have been naked, or she could have been dressed to the nines, it wouldn't have mattered. Moving gently to the song he was singing in her ear the rest of the world didn't exist. The club, Loch, and Ox, none of them were real for those few minutes. Betty was in heaven in his arms, her head on his shoulder as he sang in her ear.

She lifted her head to kiss him, soft and sweet, with an invitation for more that he seemed happy to accept. His arms tightened around her and he kissed her back. Her lips parted for his tongue and he tasted just like the whiskey he had been singing about moments before. Her hands traveled up his arms and across his shoulders then gripped his head in her hands so she could deepen the kiss and drink him in.

When he broke the kiss, Betty stared into his eyes with a dazed smile. "Bad boys aren't supposed to kiss like that." She said softly.

"And nice girls don't usually dance naked in a clubhouse, but here you are." He replied with a soft smile that made her weak in the knees.

“Well you brought me here so I guess we can blame you if I’m corrupted.” She teased. When he stiffened and stepped out of the dance, she wished that she hadn’t. “Did I say something wrong?” She asked his back as he walked away. Ox joined him, leaving her alone with Loch who was busy cleaning the last of the mess from behind the bar.

“Well, Betty, you just threw his biggest worry in his face as if it were a joke and killed his hard-on. He’ll be his cheerful self again in the morning by the time he wakes you up.” He gave her a smile. “This about makes it your bedtime, luv. Trust me, you’ll appreciate it tomorrow before you’ve had your first cup of coffee.”

“So that means that there will be coffee?” She asked while she picked up her bra and stepped into her skirt. Somehow, being alone in the room with Loch didn’t have the same effect that it did when Viper was there. It felt awkward and stilted, with none of the delirious heat there had been moments before.

“Wait, his biggest worry? About corrupting me? You’re joking right?” Betty shook her head and slid her arms into the shirt Loch had put on her earlier. She leaned against the bar while he finished and watched, trying not to notice the appealing curve of his ass in his snug jeans. “If anyone thinks that I am some innocent little school-girl then they need to check my references again.”

She rolled her eyes when he shrugged and smirked.

“Hey, it’s not my complex. He’s the one having issues. I could fuck you all night as long you’re not a virgin or looking to have babies.”

“Oh, good grief. No babies” Betty shook her head. “I can barely pay my rent, and those little things are expensive. Haven’t been a virgin since high school either.”

“Careful Betty.” Loch said, his voice huskier than it had been a moment before. “I meant what I said. I’ll fuck you until you can’t see straight if that’s what you want, but if you want Viper at the end of all this you had best take that perfect little ass upstairs to bed instead of standing here with me. If he thinks you want me more, you’ll never have him the way I think you both want.”

“What makes you think…” She didn’t get to finish asking before he put a finger to her lips.

"Shush. Don't ask stupid questions. He's my brother. I know. Plus, you've been staring at him every chance you get, like a lovestruck doe or something. I'd have to be drunk or stupid not to see it and I'm neither of those."

"So, what does that mean?" Betty asked carefully, wondering if everyone else saw what Loch did.

"That means that you're lucky that no one else is looking and that you need to go to bed. Figure out whatever feelings you have when the time comes, and the weekend is over. You're here for a job and he's the one that hired you to do it. Get it done and when the contract is up, do what comes naturally. Don't fuck it up with feelings that might not be real."

"Right. Might not be real." She said, more to herself than to him. "I think, if it's alright with you, I'll head to bed. I want to shower before I pass out."

"You do that. I'll see you at breakfast." Loch said, hitting the switch for the neon lights behind the bar. "You like bacon, Betty?"

She turned from the door to the kitchen to meet his smile.

"What kind of a question is that Loch? Of course I do, just a little crispy at the edges."

"Then I'll make sure to save you some when I cook in the

morning." He nodded to her. "Sleep well Betty."

14

Upstairs in the shower she wasn't sure if she would sleep at all. So many thoughts and emotions were flooding her brain, along with the sexual stimulation of the day and the exhaustion that went with the activities of the night. Betty had heard of being 'too tired to sleep' and now she knew what that meant. Maybe the shower would clear her head enough be able to rest.

Flicking on the light in the ensuite bathroom, Betty was amazed at the huge shower stall and the luxurious looking jet tub. The entire crew from the party could have fit in this room and she wondered if they had ever used it as a grotto for other parties.

"This is amazing." She said to herself, turning on the shower. Multiple shower heads sprung to life and steam began to rise as she brushed her hair. "What a place."

"You like it?" Called Ox's voice from the doorway.

She must have forgotten to lock the door when she came in from the kitchen.

"It was my idea." He said. "Everything is sized for me."

She smiled at him from the sink, the steam from the shower was beginning to fill the room, giving it a somewhat magical feeling that went well with the mythic looking giant man. His hair was pouring over his shoulders, across his chest like the hero in a romance movie and his eyes were twinkling at her. She took a step closer, trying to see if his eyes were blue or green.

"It looks great. I guess that would explain why I feel so tiny in here." She said, shyly touching a strand of his hair.

"You are a tiny little thing Betty." He said with a sly smile. "Which is what makes it even more impressive."

"Makes what more impressive?" She asked, hanging her towel beside the door to the shower and unfastening her robe.

"The fact that you can fit so much of me in that sweet little mouth." He said, taking the steps towards the shower with her. He pulled his shirt over his head and tossed it onto a chair. Betty couldn't believe how much she was staring. Ox towered nearly a foot above her with a physique that could only be described as Olympian. If Zeus had ever taken human form, he would have looked just like the god of a man in front of her. The sound of his jeans hitting the floor snapped her out of her stupor.

"Ox? Why are you here? Now? With me?"

"Because it's probably the only chance I'm gonna have to be alone with you all weekend and I want that." He said, stroking the back of his fingers down her cheek. "I want the chance to be with you without the rest of them staring. That okay with you?"

He stepped close to her, standing between her and the shower door while he cupped her face in his large hand. Betty searched his face while his thumb stroked her cheek, waiting for her answer. This was something almost magical, like something out of a movie. He wasn't Viper, couldn't be. He didn't have the same charm and magnetic charisma as the man that had left her downstairs but something about Ox called to her. Maybe it was that, despite his size and the reputation of his club, the big man was surprisingly gentle and sensual.

"That's okay with me Ox." She murmured, staring up at his eyes, which were an uncanny blend of blue and green together. "I'm going to shower and go to bed, which is definitely not built to your size." She teased, ducking under his arm to step into the glass enclosed shower. "You coming in?" She asked, beckoning him with the curl of her finger.

"Oh, hell yes." He stepped into the water with her and immediately pulled her to his chest.

One hand cupping her ass, lifting her just enough that their lips could easily meet. The kiss exploded with a passion that Betty was surprised she needed to express, even if it wasn't him that she felt it for.

His tongue swept against hers. He tasted like a sweet rum but smelled like leather with a hint of gasoline that was being washed away by the hot water pouring down on them. When she pushed back, taking from him as he was taking from her, Ox lifted her and stepped to press her back against the stone tile, letting her backside rest on a hand bar so they could both use their hands to explore each other.

There was no need for words between them, Betty had a feeling that he knew she wanted Viper and that, maybe, he wanted her back. This was just sex for the sake of lustful satisfaction, and it was going to be good.

Her legs wrapped around his hips and she began to rub against his growing erection. He broke the kiss with a deep growl at the contact between his shaft and her core, moving his mouth to her neck. Ox nipped and sucked, tracing lines on her neck with the tip of his tongue.

Betty moaned every time his teeth dragged across her rapidly beating pulse. She tried to move his head so she could get her mouth on him, digging her fingers into his hair to move his head, but he wouldn't let her. Ox was so intent on getting his mouth anywhere on her body he could that he wouldn't let her explore with anything but her hands. Every time she tried to move, he would bite down on her neck until she stilled and then begin to ravage her with his hands and mouth all over again. It was dizzying.

To say that Ox was an Alpha Male would have been an understatement and she loved the way he had taken complete control over the encounter. Every touch, every bite, every lick were meant to bring her pleasure and Betty was more than willing to take everything he was giving. As exciting and exhilarating as the night had been, she was craving the intimacy and solitude of just a single man, a single body, a single cock. She was overwhelmed by all the attention and, even though he was more intense than anyone else had been, Ox was making this about her in a way that made her feel as though she didn't have to put on a show. She could just be herself and revel in everything he made her feel. Oh, how he made her body feel.

After he finished feasting on her neck and shoulders Ox knelt in the shower to take one breast at a time into his mouth. The edge of his mustache and the whiskers of his beard were tickling the already sensitive flesh but the grip he had on her hips made it impossible to squirm too much.

Her hands combed through his long hair, pulling him closer and trying to find some control of the moment. She wanted to catch her breath under the falling water, but Ox was too busy, too intent on what he was doing, to let that happen.

He captured her wrists between his fingers, stilling her hands though she fought to free them.

“Now now. It’s not going to be like that.” Ox said, looking up at her with a wicked smile.

The water streaming down his face didn’t seem to bother him, though it was making her blink every time she opened her eyes.

“I want to touch you too.” She said, choking on the water. “It’s not fair if I don’t.”

He stood, towering above her in a way that should have scared her, but he excited her more than anything else, in more ways than one.

“I never said that I was going to play fair Betty.”

He grabbed a small towel from near the tap and ripped it into strips. He tossed it over another handrail above her head and then tied each end around her wrists.

“Now you’re not going to distract me, and I don’t have to worry about you letting go and falling over.” He kissed her, hard and relentless, while his hand pushed her thighs apart so his finger could tease her entrance that was already aching for him.

“Ox? Seriously?” She asked, her mouth open in delighted surprise.

His finger moving in and out of her body, while his thumb rubbed her clit, was incredible. He knew how to stir her desire. The way he was looking at her, like she was a piece of steak he was going to devour any second, made her want to claw him closer until he made her scream.

“Betty, baby, I’m gonna fuck you like a dirty girl, then clean you up and tuck you into bed.” He growled, stroking the tips of his fingers from her temple, down her throat and chest. Then he picked her up by her ass, pressing her back against the glass surrounding the shower.

“Around me.” He commanded, resulting in an instantaneous response of her legs wrapping around his waist. Betty could feel the tip of his shaft pressing slowly between her lips, stretching her as he pushed inside her.

He was so big, thick, and veined, that she wasn’t sure how much of him she could take, but she was determined to try. She wanted to feel his body slapping against hers, hear it echoing in the room along with her cries of ecstasy.

Betty worked her hips against his, trying to help him push deeper between her thighs to fill her with his delicious cock.

“Somebody’s a little bit cock starved. Aren’t you, pretty little thing?” Ox said with a grin.

Sliding one hand up her thigh he spread her legs a little

farther, angling himself in another inch. "I may have to turn you around if this is going to work the way we want it to." He grunted before lowering his head to bite her neck until she threw back her head and moaned his name.

"That's right. Get nice and loud for me." He said, pulling out of her tight core and turning her around.

Betty dragged her teeth across her bottom lip when Ox pressed his chest against her back. The hair that covered the straining muscles of his chest, and the traceable lines of his abs rubbed against her skin with an incredible friction that set even more nerves on fire than she was already trying to handle. It was going to overload every sense she had if he was able to bring her to orgasm. The way he handled her, gripping a hip and breast at the same time while bending her as far as the fabric holding her wrists would let her go, led her to believe that he wasn't going to stop until she was breathless and shaking in his arms.

"I'm going to lift you up and you're going to grab tight to that bar, Betty." He said, slowly caressing lower and lower on her body. "Gravity is going to help us, so will this." He took a small bottle from the shelf in the shower and applied the lube between her legs and over his shaft until they were both slick with it.

Carefully he adjusted his hold, guiding her body down

onto his. Inch by incredible inch Ox filled and stretched her. His rumble of satisfaction blended like a base line with the whimper that escaped her lips when his upward thrust touched his body to hers. She wanted to see him inside her, but the angles of their bodies didn't allow her to get a vantage point.

"Ox?" She gasped, rolling her hips, slowly, up, and down his shaft, milking him with her body. "I want to see you, see you inside me, but I can't from here." She called, over her shoulder at him.

"Look out the glass babe, at the mirror." He said, increasing his pace and pushing solidly into her. "See what I'm seeing."

Turning back to face the glass exterior of the shower Betty noticed a mirrored wall just opposite and, dear god, she could see everything his body was doing to hers. It was unlike anything she had ever seen; raw, erotic, and completely mesmerizing. His cock was massive and pumping in and out of her with increasing speed. His hands were steadying her body by gripping her hip and massaging her breast. He was trying to stimulate every part of her and not give her a chance to catch her breath.

It might have been a trick of the light and the steam, but Betty could have sworn she could see his cock moving inside her. Though Ox's big hands on her body could have almost covered more than her underwear, now they were making her feel exposed in an exquisitely sinful way. She had never been vain. She was always the 'funny' girl. Naked, with this giant Viking of a man buried inside her, Betty felt like the most beautiful girl in the world.

"Oh fuck, yes." Ox growled behind her, lifting her feet off the ground to pound his pulsing cock harder, deeper into her core.

Betty let her head roll back when the tension and pressure that had been building inside her began to turn to ecstasy. This was unlike anything she had ever felt before, weightless in his hands but heavy with the need for release.

"A little more. Oh, please. Just a little bit more." She begged, helplessly hanging from the handrail while her body began to explode from the inside out. "Ox! My god. Yes!"

"Atta girl, Betty. Just like that." Ox grunted. His rhythm staggering slightly while he shot his load deep into her. One hand gripped her hair, wrenching her hair back while his hips slammed against her ass one last time. "Just like that."

"Untie me, please?" She whimpered, the floating feeling was gone and her grip on the bar was slipping. "I gotta come back down to earth."

"Hold still darlin', I got you." He said, slowly easing out of her and letting her feet to the ground. "Just hold on a little longer and I'll take care of that towel too."

Betty was able to notice the water again when he stepped away from her, for the last few minutes her mind hadn't registered anything but the internal sensations. The hot water cascading down was so relaxing on her, now very sore, muscles. Each hot bead felt like part of a massage that she was desperately going to need on Monday.

Ox wrapped his arm around her waist, letting Betty rest back against him even when he let go of her so that he could cut through the soaked towel holding her arms up. Gently, with a careful slowness he lowered her arms, rubbing them to help get circulation back to normal before he cut the fabric away from her wrists completely.

"There. A little bit better?" He asked, stroking her hair from her face while Betty rubbed her wrists.

"Definitely better. That was, um, wow." Betty said, tipping her face up to catch the water. "I need to wash my hair and get some sleep, so you can, uh, go, it you want. I'll be alright." She was going to have to sit on the floor of the shower to while she washed, to make sure that she didn't fall over. She wondered how many hours of sleep she was going to get, when would they send Viper to wake her up. Viper…

what would he think of the very steamy shower she was in? Would he get jealous? Would he say anything at all?

"I'm enough of a gentleman to help you with that babe." Ox said, guiding her to the middle of the shower and easing her to the floor. "You just sit, and I'll take care of everything."

She didn't have the will or the energy to argue with him, so Betty let him move her without protest. For a rough, giant of a man he was able to move with a grace and gentility that she hadn't expected. Soon he was massaging the shampoo into her hair, tipping her head back so the soap didn't sting her eyes. He didn't say anything but was humming softly, sending the familiar song bouncing around the shower and making her smile.

"You going to sing that or just hum?" She asked, touching his thigh when she realized that he was kneeling behind her. She wanted to lean back, relax against him. She couldn't do that though, or she would fall asleep.

"Nah. I'm just going to hum it and then get you rinsed off and ready for bed." He replied, bringing her to her feet and wrapping one arm around her waist so his other hand could work the shampoo from her hair. He held a pair of bottles, by the lids, in front of her. "Vanilla or coconut conditioner?"

"Vanilla." Betty giggled at the oddity of their being such girly smells in this building full of men. She knew she was certainly not the first girl to spend time here, that didn't mean that it wasn't weird to see feminine things casually laying around amongst the aftershaves and spiced 'manly' things.

"Thanks for doing this Ox. You really didn't have to do it. I would have managed." She said, looking over her shoulder at him.

"Hey it's called 'aftercare' babe." He shrugged. "I am not going to fuck you like that and leave you in a puddle on the floor. What if you fell asleep on the floor? You'd be bitchy and sore tomorrow and it would be all my fault. Can't have that. Unless you want to have Dagger feeling like he needs to calm you down himself?"

She paused and the smile fell at the terrifying thought of being alone with Dagger. "Right. No, I don't think that would be my idea of fun. No offence to his rank, or whatever, but fear and pain isn't for me." Betty said, rising to her feet again so Ox could rinse out the sweet -smelling conditioner.

"Then let me get you tucked into bed so you can rest and be a bundle of sunshine when Viper wakes you up in the morning. I'm sure he's looking forward to that already." Ox said, turning off the taps and wrapping a surprisingly soft towel around her shoulder before scooping her up and carrying her into the bedroom.

Betty smiled and waved when he headed to the door.

"I think I am supposed to lock this for you, so no one else does what I did." He laughed and closed the door.

Betty turned off the light and lay on the bed watching the moonlight play through the trees. She wondered if Ox would get in trouble if anyone knew that he was in here? Viper hadn't said anything about not spending time alone with the members, but she wasn't eager to tell him all the same. She didn't need to tell him, not yet anyway.

With that thought, she closed her eyes and drifted off to an exhausted sleep.

15

"Wake up Betty." Viper said, putting the cup of coffee in his hand down on the bedside table so it would be the first thing that she smelled when she woke up. "It's morning, late, late morning but still. Time to wake up and come downstairs."

He smiled when the coffee did its job and she opened her eyes, taking a deep breath.

"Good morning beautiful." He said, reaching to brush a strand of hair from her eyes so he could stare into them while she focused on his face and remembered where she was. "Want to toss on a robe and come downstairs for something to eat?"

"Erm. Yeah. Uh, is that coffee?" She asked sitting up, letting the sheet fall to her lap.

The morning sunlight lit up her skin so that she was glowing like an angel in front of him, making him feel even more like a devil than he already did. Sinning with her was all he wanted to do all day and that night he intended to do just that.

"It is. Mine. If you want a cup of your very own, then you'll have to have to bring that sexy body downstairs and get it." He teased, standing up and taking a long drink of the hot, bitter liquid. It needed whiskey if he was going to get through this day without going caveman on Betty.

"Loch promised bacon. Is that in the works too?" She said, standing up and wrapping the soft black robe over her glowing curves.

He had never hated a piece of fabric so much in his life as he hated that robe.

"Yeah. I think he said something about that, and French toast. Now that is something you don't want to miss. Loch may be an asshole but he's a helluva cook."

"Ok, well, if you give me just a minute to, um, brush my hair and stuff, I'll be right down, okay?" She said, her eyes flicking towards the door on the other side of the room.

"Oh. Yeah. Sure thing." He nodded and headed to the stairs. "Don't worry, Ox is downstairs, on dish duty, so he won't interrupt you this time." He said over his shoulder, hoping that he sounded as casual as he was trying to be.

She made some tiny little squeak sound as he closed the door behind him. His boots thumped down the stairs loud enough to cover the sound of his laugh. She didn't know that the stairs and her room had video camera's for security purposes. Being the man in the office last night, he had seen the whole thing with Ox. Once he had gotten over his jealousy that the damned Viking was alone with her, he had been able to get off watching them in the shower.

She had been so helpless, suspended in the air, held up by the large and capable hands of Ox. It had been incredibly hot. She was safe enough with Ox, his heart was as big as his cock. If it had been Blades or Dagger, Viper knew that he would have intervened. They were senior members, and men he looked up to, but he was not going to let them do anything that was going to hurt or scare Betty.

If she didn't want to date him after this weekend he hoped that he'd be able to convince her to come back for the Halloween party or one of the other parties that would be going on in the next few months. It bugged Viper more than he knew how to explain, but he wanted Betty all to himself. He had to share her for the next thirty-six hours, during which he intended to have her as many times as he could.

The door at the top of the stairs closed and Betty padded down the stairs with her hair draped around her shoulders, her feet in the fuzzy slippers that Doc had assured him were 'cute'. He hadn't ever thought so before, but on her they were better than the stilettos that the strippers and other girls wore. So was the short, fuzzy, black robe that he still hated.

"Well now." He couldn't stop the grin when she smiled at him. "You look good enough to eat. Which I just might have to do after breakfast."

She blushed prettily and took the hand he offered to help her down the last few steps into the room where everyone else was gathered, eating, and enjoying morning coffee, though it was closer to lunch than breakfast.

"Morning Betty." Loch called from the stove where the smell of bacon and other breakfast food was rising. Every dick in the room rose as well when the men turned to look at the delectably tousled creature beside him.

Ox spun from the dishes so fast that he splashed water across the floor to the laughter of everyone. The room erupted with greetings from the members

"Hi there."

"Good morning."

"Hey gorgeous."

"God Ox, jumpy much?" Blades said, setting down his cup and stepping up to take Betty from Viper. He gave her a long, deep, probing kiss that would taste like the whisky disguised as coffee that the older man drank in the morning.

"Hope you slept well." He said when he let go of her. "Grab some coffee. Doc, get the girl some coffee. Loch is almost done with some fresh grub over there so make sure that you get it while it's hot."

Viper saw every man in the room, except for Ox, who had his eyes glued to the dishes, watch her walk across the room to get the hot mug of coffee. They were all treating her like they were afraid of breaking her, like cowardly teenage boys instead of men that had been fucking her brains out less than twelve hours before. He loved the fact that Ox, especially, was jumpy and awkward around her, instead of comfortable and affectionate. It showed Viper that the bigger man and Betty hadn't connected on an emotional level, despite their encounter in the shower. He was also confident that Ox knew that, official or not, Betty was Viper's girl.

She might be the 'toy' for the weekend, made obvious again by the way that Dev slipped his hand beneath the edge of her robe to give her a very different 'good morning' than the kiss from Blades, but when it was over things would be different. Maybe he was a possessive shit, or maybe he was thinking with his dick, but he wanted her all to himself.

"Hey." Interrupted Loch, to Viper's relief. "No fucking on an empty stomach. Let the woman eat first. Don't be a damned savage."

Viper found himself needing another cup of coffee, from the pot right next to the stove, and only a few feet from Betty and his brother.

"Extra bacon after a long night?" Loch asked, shooting

Betty a wink as he piled food onto her plate. "No protesting about carbs or any of that shit either." He said, dropping some French toast on her plate, smacking Viper's fingers at the same time when he reached for a piece.

"What the fuck man?" Viper said, smacking him on the arm. "I'm hungry too."

He faced off with his brother, over the frying pans on the stove. The other guys knew that they were just horsing around but Betty, innocent little thing, looked terrified that they would come to blows for real. If only she knew how close the two of them really were.

As he and Loch threw fake punches at each other, Dev and Rex cheering them on, Betty backed away with a glowing fascination in her eyes. He wondered if she was turned on by men battling it out? Some girls loved that kind of thing, even expected it in a clubhouse, but he wasn't sure if he was going to throw down with a brother just to impress a girl. He had outgrown that kind of thing a few years after high school, or at least he thought he had.

"Would you two stop acting like idiots." Dagger called, whipping a kiwi fruit across the room and nailing Loch in the side of the head.

"They can't help genetics Dagger." Ox laughed from the

dishes pit.

Loch threw the fruit at the big man and both brothers flipped Dagger the middle finger. When his brother returned to cooking Viper gestured for Betty to rejoin them, which she did with a big smile.

"You need a seat, sweetheart?" Rex called to Betty, patting his lap.

"I'm pretty happy right here by the food. Thanks though." She replied with that irresistible smile Viper liked.

"Let me help you get comfortable babe." Viper said. He picked her up by her hips and set her on the counter.

He ran his hand from her collarbone, down her chest, to her bellybutton, pushing her robe open enough to reveal the bare curves of her breasts but still keep her warm.

“Much better.” He said, handing her a freshly filled mug of coffee.

“How’re you doing?” Viper asked quietly when the others got back to their previous conversations.

“It’s all a little overwhelming in the light of day. I think I’m doing okay though I don’t know how to act now that everyone is sober and talking to me. This is unlike anything I ever even dreamed of. What do I do?” She replied in a nervous, hushed tone.

"Just treat them like a group of boyfriends. They all know about each other and most of them get off on watching you with other men just as hard as they get off when they're with you. None of them are going to get jealous and start a fight, they'll wait their turn and try to impress you. I don't see how you can lose with this setup."

Viper wondered if she noticed that he didn't include himself in any of the statements. It was hot when she was with the other members but no where near as sexy as she had looked when she had been laid out beneath his cock on the kitchcn island with Loch joining in.

"Oh, so like one of those 'reverse harem' things I've read about in books? Where there's a group of men who are all about pleasing their woman?" She said with a teasing light in her eyes.

"Well I wouldn't use that term around here. The boys aren't going to take to it all that well. They'd likely say that it was the kind of reverse harem with one girl and many, many men who will make fun, nasty, kinky demands of her." He leaned closed to whisper in her ear while she started to eat the syrup covered bread and bacon. "They're going to enjoy you, one at time, two and a time and, if you're a very, very good girl, you'll get three hard cocks filling you up again."

Her eyes widened and her entire body blushed, so he slid

his arm around her waist. Leaning against the edge of the counter, holding his coffee in his other hand so that he didn't slide it between her gloriously soft thighs to play with her pussy.

"After we eat, there are a few guys going to clean the kitchen, probably Ox and Dev, Doc is supposed to clean and prep the bar for tonight and the rest of us; Loch, Blades, Dagger, Rex and I, we're all going to the hot tub. I want you to join us for some fun. What do you think? Can you handle the five of us in the water?"

She turned her head to look at him, her face close enough he could have kissed her with just the turn of his head.

"I can handle all of you." She whispered back.

The emphasis that she put on the word 'you' sent a bolt of heat to his cock. If it wasn't for the risk of someone else joining in, he would have tugged her just a little closer and slid her hips just far enough off the edge that he could thrust inside her. She would ride him while he stripped the robe off her shoulders and dropped it on the floor before they joined it and he pounded her into the tile. She would be scratching his back, her legs wrapped around him while she screamed his name, again and again. If they were alone.

"I don't know if you could, if I let loose on you the way I

would if there was no one else here." He growled back, hungry for something that wasn't on the stove-top.

"Are you going to teach me a lesson Viper?" Betty purred.

Their eyes locked and Viper watched her hand sneak across the counter, over the edge so that she could cup his erection through his jeans.

"You going to teach me a lesson with this Viper?" She asked with a playfully innocent voice.

Fuck. He was in trouble, but two could play that game.

"If I were alone, I'd give you more than just a lesson, Betty."

He snapped his jaw at her and winked.

"Not right now though."

"Is that a threat Viper, or a promise?" She asked him.

He groaned, the way she was rubbing him through his jeans was going to cause a few problems if he didn't stop her though he really, really, didn't want to make her stop.

"You can take that as a promise."

They stared at each other for a minute and he could have sworn the sounds from the other seven men talking dimmed while he memorized the excited little smile she was wearing.

"Well, if I'm spending some time in the water with you fellas, I should go get something on."

"You know that we're just going to take a bikini right off, don't you?" Viper asked, raising a brow as she hopped from the counter, her hand on his chest to steady herself on the heels of the fuzzy pornstar slippers.

"Who said it was a bikini." She said huskily, walking past him and back towards the door to her room.

The whole room had quieted to hear that parting phrase and, as soon as the door closed behind her, there was more than a few whistles of appreciation.

“You seem to have a way with that one, Viper.” Blades said, taking a drink. “Something special going on? Putting down a claim?”

He wanted to say yes, tell every one of them to keep their hands off her and their cocks in their pants, but that would be stupider than even he was. If he tried to lay claim to her, in the middle of a party like this, they would all spend the rest of the weekend doing everything they could to keep them apart. Every single one of them would enjoy fucking his girl. Not because they wanted her more, or because they had any special grudge against him; it would simply be a case of punishing him for taking something away from the club before they were finished with her.

"No. Nothing special and no claims. Just gotta treat her like a woman instead of a blow-up doll that talks." He teased back, setting off a round of comparisons between live women and toys before the men allotted to chores got to work and the other five, including Viper, headed out to the hot tub.

It was giving off steam in the cool air and the view from the deck, over the ravine with a river rushing across the bottom and the foothills of the Rocky Mountains just beyond that, was one of Viper's favorite things about this place. If it wasn't the clubhouse and had just been a regular lodge, run by some interfering old couple that had lived 'in the area' all their lives, he would have taken a girl like Betty here for a weekend getaway just based on the view alone. The fact that there was great fishing in the river didn't hurt things either, neither did the hunting in the fall.

He stripped down with the others and got into the water, waiting for Betty to arrive with a cup of coffee in his hand. He tried to pretend that he was interested in what the others were saying while he waited for the real fun to arrive. The water wasn't the only reason Betty was going to be getting hot and wet. Viper fully intended to get his hands all over her, especially after the show in the shower the night before.

Loch was right in the middle of a hunting story from the

year before when he claimed to have lost 'the biggest buck in the mountain' to a cougar when the door to the house closed with a bang causing every head in the tub to turn. Viper smiled at the sight of her walking towards them, looking like a goddess wrapped in the same black robe she had gone upstairs in. He could tell she was up to something by the way she was smiling at him.

Loch nudged him in the ribs.

"You're staring with a grin like a birthday clown, dumbass."

"Did someone say birthday?" Betty said, arriving at the pool and dropping the robe to the ground to reveal what she had changed into for the pool time.

16

Viper couldn't take his eyes off Betty. The only thing she was wearing was a silver body chain and a smile that was getting brighter every second.

He remembered buying that particular chain, but he hadn't considered what it would look like looping underneath the full, round breasts that overflowed in his hands and across hips that were shaped for his hands alone. He wanted to follow every shining silver link with his mouth, especially the ones between her legs. The memory of that sweet honeypot was fresh enough in his mind to make his mouth water immediately.

"You look…" He couldn't finish the sentence. He couldn't think of a word that could describe how amazing she looked.

"He means to say that you look good, good and cold." Loch said, standing before Viper could find his footing in the water. "Why don't you come in here and show that off just a little bit better, hm?"

As soon as she was in the water Viper reached out and pulled her into his lap. He had been going to put her beside him until he had seen her naked.

"Comfy?" He rumbled in her ear. He wrapped an arm

around her waist and pulled her snug up against his own naked body. She fit like she was made for him and his dick didn't take long to respond to her bottom pressing close enough that it would only take a subtle shift of both their hips to make this a much more intimate encounter.

"Oh, I feel just fine Viper." She said over her shoulder. "And so do you." She whispered with a wink and a roll of her hips just to finish getting him hard as a rock.

"Are you sure his lap isn't a bit boney for you girl?" Blades called from the other side of the tub, lighting up a cigar and pouring more bourbon into his mug. "I don't have that washboard him and Loch are sporting but I'm a bit comfier to sit on."

"I think I'm good right here but maybe I'll come sit with you if I get…uncomfortable." She replied with a wiggle that almost sent Viper into a state of euphoria.

"Not in the next few minutes." He said, tightening his hold on her. "I don't mind being your throne for a little while if you want to be my dirty princess."

"Don't princesses wear pearls and crowns?" Rex asked, cracking open the first beer of the day.

"I'll give her a pearl necklace alright." Dagger said, his eyes riveted to Betty's chest while his hand slid below the water. “Just slide on over girlie and rub it out. You’ll look good covered in me.”

“You’re dreaming old man.” Loch said, gesturing for a beer from Rex. “Can’t you tell? Little brother has a pair of fingers in that pussy already.”

When he nodded to Viper who slowly moved his hand deeper between Betty’s legs and began to play between her folds.

“He’s right Dagger.” Viper added. “I’m firmly of the opinion that the woman should really cum first. Several times if possible.”

“We all know that really isn’t how you like to play though, right Dagger?” Loch said to the senior member while he casually reached over to play with one of Betty’s, soft, ripe breasts as though it was the most natural thing in the world for him to do on an early Saturday afternoon.

When her back arched, pressing her chest into Loch’s hand Viper slid a pair of fingers inside her, stroking and teasing, playing her for her own pleasure as well as his own impending gratification.

“You see, fellas, she needs to get a fix of her own before she’ll be ready to play with the big boys over there. Isn’t that right Betty?” Loch asked, sliding right next to Viper.

The brothers shared a smile and nod that they both understood completely. If they were going to keep the girl from the hands, and cock of Dagger it was going to have to be a team effort, and a hell of a show.

Betty nodded, her teeth dragging across her bottom lip while they continued to stimulate her senses with their hands, mouths, and any part of their bodies they could get into full contact with her skin.

"You're right Loch. Oh, so right." She moaned breathily, pressing her hips down towards Viper's cock while she leaned forward into his brother's hands. "I really want, I need, to get off. It'll feel so good. Please?"

She was begging and it was as sweet as music to his ears. Viper was rock hard behind her, throbbing between her ass cheeks. If they weren't in the water his shaft would be weeping with the need to be inside her.

"The poor thing sounds delirious with the need, doesn't she?" Rex said, taking a second beer before settling back to enjoy the show that the trio was putting on.

"I think you boys ought to do whatever is needed to get that pretty girl ready for what I have planned for tonight. Take the edge off before the tournament." Blades said with a laugh.

"Boss says please the lady, little brother." Loch said with a smile that Viper joined.

“You’re a fucking ass, Loch. Call me that again and I’ll stop sharing with you.”

“I’m the ass?” Loch laughed, pinching Betty’s nipples until she squirmed again. “You’re the one in position to take that particular hole. I think that might be exactly what Betty needs.”

Viper felt her still on his lap when Loch took her chin in his hand. “What do you think Bets? Do you want Viper to fuck that sweet little ass of yours while I play with all you’re offering me here?” He palmed a breast with one hand and used the other to take her hand from Viper’s thigh, where her nails had been digging into his skin, and placed it on his own cock. “Want a triple dose of pleasure again? The three of us working your body together until we’re all satisfied?”

As soon as her head nodded Viper watched her sweet lips close around Loch’s thumb the same way she took a cock between them.

“Yes please. Right now?” She whispered hoarsely.

“As the lady says, Viper. As the lady says.” Blades nodded from the far side of the hot tub. All three of them were getting ready to enjoy the show.

“Don’t look at them now Betty. Just watch Loch and feel

me. Relax and enjoy every sensation I'm going to give you." Viper said, lifting her off his lap just enough to give him space to get into position and slick some lube over his cock and the sweet little hole he was about to plunder.

Loch's hands took over holding her, his cheekiest smile working to reassure Betty that everything was fine and that she was going to enjoy this as much as she had enjoyed them in the kitchen.

Focusing on his own body when he knew that she was being handled Viper positioned himself at her back entrance. Slowly, with achingly careful pressure he worked his cock, slowly, between her cheeks until she was filled with him. Only when she was pressed firmly against him did her ease back into the water.

Then Loch put his hand over her wrist, her hand was still wrapped around his dick, and began to show her the rhythm he liked. The wicked shine in his eyes saying that the small hand around him had a stronger grip than anyone would guess.

Viper had been carefully increasing his pace, rolling her hips against him, doing his best to not turn into a savage minded bastard. He could not have imagined how tight she would be around him, or how incredible it would feel, different than anyone he had ever had before.

Together the trio was creating a bond built on the simplest and yet most complicate feeling: pleasure. This was the third time in less than twelve hours that they had been with her together. Viper wondered, for a second, if his brother was developing feelings for her too? That thought disappeared when Loch whispered a name that was definitely not the name of the girl milking his cock with her hand while he kept his eyes closed, at the edge of bliss.

"Go for the Eiffel Tower." Dagger called, exhaling from the cigar that he had lit while Viper had been focused on burying himself in Betty's ass.

Loch opened his eyes at the not so subtle command from the senior member. Viper, nudging deeper inside Betty, flicked his eyes from his brother to the head of the girl between them. Viper gave a single shake of his head when Loch tilted his head to ask, wordlessly, if that was what he wanted. She wasn't ready for that kind of thing and he wasn't going to push her to please Dagger and his dark fantasies.

"No time for towers today Dagger." Loch said, putting his hand on Betty's, craning his neck back. "I think you boys should all enjoy the girl's handiwork. It's unlike anything I've had in a long time."

He grunted, letting go to the rhythm of Betty's strokes.

Viper could feel the tension in her body, the need for a release of her own. He kept one hand on her hip but slid the other back between her thighs to tease her clit until she was trembling in the aftermath of her orgasm.

"Such a good girl you are, Betty, to put on a show like that for us." Viper said, biting the side of her neck until she reached up and raked her fingernails up his arm as she moaned his name.

Loch sat on the edge of the tub, taking a swig of his beer and gesturing to the others to step up.

"I mean it fellas. Let her get those hands on you and tell me she's not something special." He said, leaning back to catch the sun all over his completely naked body.

Betty was staring, still gasping for breath after a second orgasm at the tips of his fingers. "Would one of you get over here so she can stop staring at Mr. Show-Off over there?" Viper called with a laugh that almost turned to something else when she started to grind herself up and down his shaft.

"Looks like you really do need a distraction Betty." Blades said, standing in the water to make his way over to where she was impaled and writhing. "Dagger, the woman has two hands, get over here and have some fun." He called to the other member, who moved to join them at a slow and easy pace.

Dagger and Blades were either oblivious to the fact that Betty was uncomfortable with both of them or they were ignoring it. Viper could tell, by the way her breathing changed and how her body tensed, that there was something about this pair that was making her nervous.

It was admirable how she was playing the game of cock tease and seductress. It might have been believable to the casual observer bit Viper was anything but the casual observer. He was doing his best to reassure her of her safety with his touch, under the water where no one could see. As the men got more excited, more stimulated, by the woman sitting on his cock Viper looked towards his brother. He was grateful to see that he had his eyes on the pair as well. With the pair of them both looking out for Betty, she would be as safe as possible.

Dagger had just reached out to take hold of Betty's head, gripping her hair firmly as he hissed between his teeth, when a cell phone on the far side of the water rang. Rex, who had been adding to the waves in the water with the motion of his hand, stopped so he could hand the phone to Dagger.

"Yeah…okay…shit." He said into the device, stepping back from Betty and gesturing for Blades to join him as he hung up the phone. "Satan is coming, tonight, for the tournament."

"Oh fuck." Blades turned and left the tub. "You lot finish up…whatever you're going to do and get things ready for a big-time visit."

"Who is Satan, exactly?" Rex asked, grabbing a towel, and following the others out of the water. "I've heard the name but never had a chance to meet him. No one really talks about him."

Loch cursed quietly and rolled his eyes. "Satan is the son of Samuel Rathbourne, our president."

"Satan?" Betty asked, from the water as Viper carefully moved her to the space beside him so that he could join the others in preparing for the arrival of the VIP. "Isn't that a bit of overkill?"

"Oh, the irony of it isn't lost on anyone." Viper said with a smile, handing her back the robe she had been wearing earlier. "His father has a wicked sense of humor and Satan is just…"

"He's a damn good time when he wants to be." Loch finished the sentence. "If he's coming then tonight will be more than just a few drinks around the bar. This is going to be something special if he's coming down for the night."

Viper and Loch helped Betty out of the water and walked,

slowly, back to the house. The trio felt strangely natural, and he was enjoying it more than he should.

"If he is so important does that mean that, when he's here, I'm just for him?" Betty asked, just before they got to the door.

"Well normally." Loch said, before Viper interrupted.

"But not tonight. The tournament is what he's coming for, not you. I'm sure he'll want you, who wouldn't with how I'm going to get you done up. As far as you're concerned, he is just like any other member."

"Yeah any other member with more hair than all the rest of us except for Ox." Loch added. "He's also got access to more money than God, and if he likes you then, he'll spend a lot of it on you."

"Oh." She wrinkled her nose in a way that made Viper want to kiss her again. "Well money, like a lot of money, has always made me uncomfortable so that's not going to help him. What kind of tournament is it exactly? Why is he coming?"

Viper opened the door to show the other men sliding something across the floor from the garage.

"Pool, and you'll be the prize."

17

Hours later, the sun was setting, and the guys were waiting on the arrival of the man they called Satan and The Devil. Betty was getting a little bit nervous.

She looked amazing and every time she glanced in the mirror behind the bar, she was surprised by the taste in clothes of whichever member did the shopping. The dress was blood red and shimmery without the irritation of sequins. It was cut low between her breasts and held up by thin bejeweled straps. It fit like it was painted on her and was just long enough that she could sit on it, but she definitely felt the need to keep her knees together whenever there was someone sitting across from her.

It seemed as though a few of the guys were on edge and she kept wondering what it was about him that seemed to scare even Dagger. Was he going to be like a movie villain? With piercings and tattoos? Or was he going to be a surprise like Viper, Loch and Ox were?

The brothers were taking turns between the bar and serving the drinks that the men at the pool tables were ordering. For some reason they weren't starting the tournament until the VIP arrived.

"Is he bringing a prize or something?" She asked, taking a

sip of the rum and coke that Viper had made for her. She never had to ask for a refill, he was ready with a freshly filled glass just as she was finishing the one in her hand.

"Well he's bringing the cash prize." Loch said, taking a pair of beers from the counter. "But you're the grand prize Betty. Didn't Viper tell you that?"

"Shut up you idiot." Viper growled. "I was getting to it."

"Well you might want to tell her soon, little brother." Loch snapped back. "He's is going to be here any minute and the lady shouldn't be unaware of what that plan for the night is, especially since she is a big part of all the fun."

"Ass." Viper muttered while Loch walked away.

Betty wondered if they had been fighting while she had been upstairs resting and getting ready. They had been a united duo when they had gotten out of the hot tub, but now they seemed more likely to start throwing fists at each other than anyone else.

"Don't mind those two, Betty." Ox said with a warm smile. Taking the seat next to her he easily lifted her onto his lap. "They fight likes dogs with a bone at the best of times. it's different tonight, because of Satan. No one was really expecting that he would show up."

He lowered his voice to a whisper while his palms ran up

and down her leg. “I don’t think that everyone is ready for him either.”

“What does that mean?” Betty asked, leaning back against his broad, bare, chest.

“It means he shouldn’t be talking about club stuff. Not tonight and not with you.” Viper snapped, slapping a glass down on the counter.

“You know better.” He said to Ox, who wrapped an arm around Betty as he shrugged.

Betty looked at Viper, he was doing his best not to look at her, his eyes on the door. She wondered if he had gotten in trouble for something because of her.

“What was the fight about?” She whispered to Ox, turning her head to look at him, placing small, soft, kisses along his neck. If she was going to play the part she was brought here to play, especially if she was meant to be a prize tonight, she couldn’t let herself get caught up on the drama of the club since that wasn’t her life, or her business.

“About tonight. Viper isn’t supposed to play in the tournament, but he wants a shot at the grand prize. Loch tried to talk sense into him, of course it didn’t work.” Ox said. “He’s too stubborn.”

“What’s the big deal about the grand prize? Why isn’t he

allowed to play pool? Isn't the whole group going to play?" She asked, stroking a hand down his long hair.

"He used to play for money and win. Viper was, and still could be, one of the best pool sharks in the country. He had to head to Canada for a few years because he won too much money from the wrong people."

"So, he's unbeatable and he's playing…to win me?" She asked, trying to hide her surprise at the actions of the man who still wouldn't look at her.

"That is his plan. Unless Satan tells him that he can't when he gets here. That's what everyone is waiting for. To see if it's going to come down to the two of them, head to head for the…well, for you."

"Who do you think is going to win? Is this new guy really that good?" Betty asked, reaching for another fresh drink Viper had just slid across the bar where she had been positioned, naked, the night before.

"I learned the hard way, a long time ago, not to bet against Viper when it comes to pool or women."

"Then he really wants to win that cash." She said, mostly to herself, as she took a sip of the drink.

Ox's hand slid between her legs when she settled back onto his lap. The way he was playing with her body was almost as comforting as it was stimulating. His fingertips were calloused which gave her a rough, tickle before the sensation turned into pleasure. His mouth was on her shoulder: kissing, nipping, and licking.

"I don't think it's the cash he's wanting to win Betty." He whispered in her ear, his voice dropping to a low rumble that she could feel in his chest.

She was about to ask if he thought that Viper was willing to risk trouble with the other members because he wanted to win her, in whatever capacity they had planned for her as a prize, when the main door of the house slammed open and a leather clad man stepped inside. Silencing the room.

His helmet was still on when he turned to face the pool tables, so Betty got to drink in the long legs in the leather bike chaps and the jacket with a black and white crow skull emblazoned on the back. When he pulled the helmet off Betty was surprised to see his shoulder length blonde hair and when he turned around, he had a face like a Dolce and Gabbana model. She couldn't tell what was more surprising, the bright blue eyes or the warm smile on his face as he strode across the room to meet her.

"Stand up and show him what you're made of." Ox said in her ear, slipping out from underneath her as Satan approached.

“You must be Betty.” He said, throwing his arms around her the exact same time she had moved to shake his hand, which pressed her hand right into his crotch.

“Sorry. Yes, I am. Sorry about that. I am Betty. Nice to meet you.” She was stammering and nervous, not just because her hand was still on his leather clad erection either. His smile was the kind that dazzled women into brainless idiots, which she wasn’t, though she certainly felt like one in that moment.

“Well, Betty, if you’ll let go of my cock for a little while I’m going to have a drink and play some pool with these fine brothers of mine and then, if I win, you and I can have all night to get to know each other a lot better than we do right now.”

He dropped a quick kiss on her cheek, as if they were old friends instead of complete strangers that had just had the most awkward meeting possible. She watched him walk to the tables where the members were waiting to greet the son of their president.

Ox and Loch had already joined the group, but Viper was still behind the bar. The way that the others were looking over towards her, Betty had the feeling that she was expected to join them, but she wasn’t ready. She didn’t want to go without Viper. Even though he seemed a little bit indifferent now she still felt as though he was the safest person in the building.

"You coming? Or did Satan's charisma root you to the ground? He does that." Viper said, suddenly appearing beside her, his hand on her backside and his lips at her ear. He was so close she could smell him over every other scent in the room.

"No. He's just not what I was expecting." She turned to smile at him, hoping that he would smile back. "He isn't like the rest of you. He's nothing like you at all." She added, stepping towards the tournament with him.

"Would you want him to be? Should he be scary? A bit of a monster like Dagger?"

"No, I've had enough monsters in my past. I'm looking for something different."

"You're not going to find any white knights here, Betty." He said standing around the pool table, directly opposite Satan, as Dev and Doc worked on their game. "We're all demons in our own way."

"Demons can be heroes too." She said, putting her arms around his waist and pressing a few kisses to the back of his hoodie. It was an unconscious decision to be bold and make the statement that he couldn't or wouldn't, she wanted to be his.

His hand rested on top of hers on his belt. It seemed so natural that she sighed, wishing that it were just the two of them playing pool together. Instead there was eight other men, and only four of them were focused on the tables.

"Since when are demons heroes, Betty? We're one bad day away from monsters ourselves." He said softly, turning his head so that the others couldn't see his face, but she could.

"There's a whole book series on just that. Immortal men possessed by demons." She stared up into the dark chocolate of his eyes. "Handsome man saves me from the monsters."

"Handsome man saves you from the monsters?" He said, arching a brow with a smirk.

"Heard it on a tv show once and knew that was what I needed." She said, vaguely aware that Doc won the game and that Rex and Ox were almost finished the game at the second table.

"Why are you telling me this Betty?" He asked darkly.

The tone of his voice sent chills down her spine but, as the next pair of games was set up and Loch headed towards Viper with a pair of cues, she knew she couldn't back down now.

"Because you're the most handsome man I've ever met and I think you can save me from any monsters I'm going to find, here or anywhere else."

“Viper.” Loch called, tossing him the pool cue. “You and Ox. Table one. Dagger and I are on table two.”

She watched him walk to the far end of the table without answering her and she wondered if she had said too much. Did men like him even care about that kind of thing or was it just sexual chemistry?

"You and Viper?" A soft voice chuckled in her ear. Betty turned her head to find Satan standing beside her with a cocky smile on his face

“What? No. I just met him two days ago." She answered with an uncertain smile when Satan ran his knuckle down her arm.

"Really? I would have thought you two were together." He reached out to take her glass and sipped the cocktail with a shake of his head that sent his blond hair flying around his face.

"Oh sweetheart, you'll never get drunk with that.” He said then rushed over to the bar and grabbed the rum bottle. He poured at least three shots worth into her glass. "There. That's a proper party drink." He said, gesturing for her to drink. His grin turned into a laugh when she sputtered at the strength of the burn.

"That's, wow, that's strong." Betty said when she could

talk. When she glanced around the room, she was surprised to see Viper glaring at the man beside her. "You're going to get me drunk."

"Well that's the point of a party. To have a little fun." He slid his arm around her shoulder, the tips of his fingers playing with the strap of her dress. "You need to relax, enjoy the night."

She gave him a smile, trying to relax even though she could practically feel the jealousy radiating off Viper when Satan settled next to her, his hands in constant contact with her skin.

"So, who do you think is going to be against me in the final round?" Satan asked her, after gesturing for her to sit next to him at the tall table between the two pool tables.

18

She felt exposed underneath the brightest light in the room, which made her dress shine even more. When he rested his hand on her thigh and Viper narrowed his eyes Betty realized exactly what Satan was trying to do.

Someone had told the new man that Viper wanted her, and the blonde was using her to try and distract him so that he would lose the game and get eliminated from the tournament.

"I've been told that only a fool would bet against Viper. If you're going to win, you'll have to play against him and try to beat."

Behind her there was a sharp laugh and Betty turned to see Loch looking at her with approval in his eyes before he winked and toasted her with his drink.

"You don't think that I can beat Viper?" Satan asked. "You've got a lot of confidence in a man you hardly know."

"I trust that he's as good as his brothers say he is. They may be many things, but these guys are not liars, especially when they're praising each other."

"You're right about that." He laughed and poured more rum into her glass.

It was almost completely rum now and she was starting to

feel it. She was glad that she was sitting at the table since both pool tables were starting to spin just a little bit. As far as she could tell Dev had won against Doc and Blades had utterly defeated Rex.

"Why aren't you playing yet? Are you so good that you get to skip a round?" She asked, blinking into the glass, and wishing she could have walked across the room to get water, but she didn't trust her balance.

"I'm the best there is sweetheart." Satan said with a smugness that she could still hear through the alcohol haze. "That's why we're going to be cuddle buddies later when I win this thing."

"Wait? What? Cuddle buddies? You and me? How does that get to happen?" She asked, slapping the glass on the tabletop.

"When I beat your boyfriend in the final match, if he makes it that far, he's going to escort you and me upstairs to that bedroom, then go sit in his little security office and watch the hours of fun we have together, naked."

She looked up at him and was disturbed to find the good-natured jokester gone and in his place was a man with a serious and vengeful expression.

"Why do you want to hurt him so badly?" She asked in a

hiss, completely unaware that Viper's game had finished, and Ox had lost badly to the superior skilled man that was now stalking his way around the table towards her and Satan.

"How drunk did you get her man? Can she even stand up straight?" Viper snarled, picking up the glass to smell the rum. "Dev, go get a bottle of water, sealed. Bring a few of them for Betty so she can get sober enough to know what's going on around her."

"Why don't I take her with me and sit in the room with her?" Dev relied, holding out a hand to Betty.

"No way. She stays in sight of everyone until she's sober enough to know what she's doing and why." Viper said, looking towards Blades for his permission to go against the son of their president who was standing with a smug look on his face.

When he got the nod that he needed Viper led her towards the couch and made sure she started drinking the bottled water as soon as Dev brought it over.

"Just drink up and we'll get you something to eat too. You're too small to drink straight rum like that."

"I'm alright. You can go play." She said, putting her hand on his chest, just above the zipper, where she could feel his heart beating. It didn't matter that there were still men watching both her and the game between Loch and Dagger, he was all she cared about. His heartbeat and scent were just as intoxicating as the alcohol and she wanted to submerge herself in him and get lost for hours.

“I’ll sit right here while Dagger and Loch finish.” He said with a softer smile than she had seen from him all night. “I have nothing else I need to worry about, except keeping you safe.”

“That’s good of you Viper, to keep my little teddy bear warm and safe. I’ll play Dev and Ox while we wait for Dagger and Loch to figure out their game.”

"You're going to stay with me? You don't have to." Betty said, letting her head rest against his chest. "You have to win so I don't have to sleep next to him." She said softly, hoping no one else could hear her.

"Don't worry Betty. I'm not going to lose to Blades or Satan." He pressed a kiss to the top of her head. "You'll be with me tonight. I'll be in shit tomorrow morning, but you'll be mine tonight."

She wanted to say something else, but he handed her another bottle of water.

"Drink up and I'll get you something to eat." He got up and nodded to Ox. "Stay with her and don't move until I'm back."

He ordered before disappearing into the kitchen.

Betty looked around, her head was clearing a little, she was relieved to see Satan deeply involved in a game with Rex.

"Don't let him get to you." Ox said, putting his arm around her shoulder.

"Viper? I'd like him to get to me."

He laughed. "No. Satan. That's an old rivalry you're in the middle of."

"What happened? Why would he try to use me to get to him?" If she were a little more sober, she was sure it would all make sense, but something wasn't adding up.

"Because Satan hates to lose at anything and the only person who can beat him, with women or pool is Viper."

"So, I'm just a pawn in their contest." Her heart sank a little.

"For Satan, absolutely. I've never seen him serious about anything or anyone except winning."

"What about Viper?" She asked, reaching for another bottle of water, and starting to feel clearer.

"I'm not sure if I can answer that, but you'll find out for yourself when he wins."

“You seem really sure that he's going to win this. You guys didn't rig it, did you?"

"There's no way we could rig it without one of them figuring it out. I have a hundred bucks riding on his victory, so I bloody well hope he wins" Ox said with the shake of his head as he pulled her closer so that he could tease her inner thigh with his fingers.

It struck Betty how the big man seemed to be more focused on her pleasure than his own whenever they were alone together.

"Why don't you have a girlfriend Ox?”

“Well this lifestyle doesn’t always make that kind of thing easy. I never know when a woman likes me until she’s already over me and someone points out why she stopped talking to me. I’m pretty much a dumbass.”

“Nah, you’re a nice guy." She said as one of the games ended with Loch winning against a very annoyed Dagger.

"So, who plays next?" She asked, unable to stop her smile as Viper pushed open the doors from the kitchen and brought her a plate of grilled cheese sandwiches.

"Me against Loch and Satan against Blades." Viper said, handing her the plate.

"Hey Ox, get behind the bar. I think we all need some

shots for the semifinals." Dagger said as he left the table.

Betty watched all three of the men she trusted to keep her safe walk away to either the pool tables or the bar. That meant Betty was alone on the couch, finishing her food as Dagger stood over her with a smile that made her skin crawl.

"You ready to get back to the party Missy?"

She swallowed hard and stood up, forcing herself not to flinch when he took her arm and led her away from the pool tables and back towards the bar.

"I'm sure Ox isn't as good a bartender as Viper, but he can make a few shots for us to enjoy, to toast the tournament." His hand slid to her ass and squeezed. "I didn't win the grand prize, but I think you and I should have a bit of fun together during the last game, don't you?"

“Well, we could do that.” Betty replied nervously, watching Ox mix the shots. She caught a reflection in the mirror that showed both brothers keeping their eyes on her whenever they weren’t shooting their game. “But I’m pretty sure that I’m not supposed to, since I’m supposed to be the prize of the night.”

“Neither one of them is going to appreciate sloppy seconds, Dagger.” Rex pointed out.

“Who the hell asked you?” Dagger growled, standing

behind Betty, his hand on either side of her trapping her body between him and the bar. The hand that had been on her ass was now creeping its way around the edge of her dress and dipping beneath the edge to try and get a more intimate grip on her. "Me and Betty haven't had any time to play yet, she's been too busy treating you boys like you're the big deal around here. What do you say Betty? Time to earn that hefty paycheck by putting your ass into it."

She wasn't supposed to say 'no' to anything that wouldn't leave a mark or actually hurt her. She was supposed to be at the disposal of every member present when she wasn't in the room they had assigned to her, but everything in her body was screaming at her to run as far from Dagger as she could. The only reason she wasn't fighting him right now was that the struggle would distract Viper and make him lose the game she so desperately wanted him to win.

"Dagger, I don't want to get in trouble. I'm supposed to go back and sit with the guys playing. They're watching right now so I should really do that shot and get back."

She hoped that it worked, that he would let her go, but he laughed in her ear.

"Ox, two shots for the little fuck toy here. Rex, go get the red room ready. Betty and I are going to have a little…cuddle time."

His hand grabbed between her legs, his fingers probing for more, and she couldn't help but scream and push hard enough against the bar that she could duck out from his trap.

"No!" She backed away from him, shaking her head. "Not going to happen. Not you and not alone. No."

She heard pool cues clattering to the floor and two pairs of booted feet running across the room. Viper and Loch were suddenly between her and the fuming Dagger.

"I think the lady doesn't want to play with you, Dagger" Viper growled. His hands were clenched in tight fists while he blocked Betty from the sight of the other man.

"I don't give a damn what the bitch wants. I'll have my cock satisfied and you're not going to get in my way, Viper. Move. It's what we're paying her to do. Now I can do it in private, or you can watch, but I'm going to fuck that tight little pussy of hers right now."

Betty yelped in fear when he tried to push his way past the brothers. Her blood was racing, and she was legitimately thinking about hitting Dagger with the heel of her shoes if he came any closer.

"You two don't have the authority to stop me. Get out of the way or I'll be dealing with both of you out back in the woodshed tomorrow morning."

She didn't know what he meant but it couldn't be a good thing. Loch looked over his shoulder at her while Viper kept his eyes firmly on Dagger.

"You're not going to touch her if she says no. I know the kind of twisted shit you're into and you're not doing that with her."

"You arrogant little shit. I'm going to…"

"You're not going to do a thing." Satan said calmly, joining the group. "Except leave. You're not to come back to the house until my father decides that you're allowed. Get out, now."

Everyone in the room stood still until Dagger had left the building and fired up his bike outside. Once he was off the property the remaining men all looked at each other.

"One last game for the grand prize?" Satan said to Viper, who had his eyes locked on Betty. "You and me, like last time?"

19

Viper looked from Satan to Betty. She was staring at him with those big eyes full of gratitude and lingering traces of fear. He didn't want to play the damned game, what he wanted was to take her upstairs and kiss away every drop of terror in those beautiful eyes.

There was only one way that was going to happen. He had to win.

"Rack 'em up Ox. I've got a game to win."

Satan chuckled when the big man moved from behind the bar to set up the final match.

"You sure you're ready to take me on again, Viper?" Satan said with a grin. "You're not too distracted by those big eyes and that tight little dress?"

"I got my eyes on the prize and I'm going to thoroughly enjoy kicking that leather clad ass of yours." Viper said with a smirk.

He slid an arm around Betty's waist, pulling her and those delectable, shimmering curves tight against him.

"Kiss for luck babe?" He asked, hoping that Dagger hadn't just killed the entire weekend with his stupid assault.

He held his breath until she smiled and wrapped her arms

around his neck.

“You can have it, but you don’t need it. Not really.” She said, beaming at him with what looked like gratitude.

When this was done, he was going to change that gratitude back to the passion that had been there before.

He tipped her chin up just enough that her eyes would see nothing but his.

“I need whatever you can give me.” He whispered back before taking her mouth in a kiss.

It started out soft, begging for a reaction. When she pressed back, he tightened his hold and deepened the kiss with a thrust of his tongue. He had to taste her before heading to the table.

He could vaguely hear the clattering of the balls but was so deep in the kiss that he didn’t hear anything else, notice anything else, until Loch put his hand on his shoulder.

“Hey lover-boy.” He said with a laugh. “If you don’t intend to forfeit then you’d better get started. You and I both know that Satan will still take your girl, and he won’t share like I do.”

The rest of the members chuckled, while Blades shook his head and jerked his thumb towards the table.

"Go make me proud, boy." He said. "We'll talk about the rest of this tomorrow."

With a wink and a kiss to her forehead Viper turned to head to the table where Satan was waiting for him, taking a long draught from the beer Ox handed him.

"Come watch me play to Betty, then we'll go upstairs and play until you cum, again and again. I want to hear a very different scream from you."

"Maybe I'm the one that's going to make you scream. Ever think of that Viper?" She sassed back at him, sending him to the game with a laugh.

Facing Satan across the green velvet of the pool table, Viper glared at the long-haired leather clad jackass.

"You really think I'm going to let you have her? That you can actually win this, against me?" He said, chalking the tip of his cue.

"You really think I'm not going to annihilate you after the last time we did this? Do you even remember her name? The girl you won, fucked, then drove out of the clubhouse and the city? I still can't find her. You're the one who took her from me and now I am going to take your pretty little Betty. She's coming upstairs with me tonight and out of here with me tomorrow when I leave. Let's see how you like looking for the one woman you want, knowing that you're never going to find her."

Betty was staring, shock on her face. While Viper was starting to get pissed at the pretty boy who thought he could come here and make a mess of things with the first girl in years he actually wanted to date.

"She wanted to get away from you, like any woman who's had to put up with you. I just helped with what she wanted." He said, taking his first shot.

"Well, want it or not, when I win this Betty is coming with me for a little out of town holiday."

"That's kidnapping." Betty objected from the other end of the table. "I didn't sign on for that."

"Quiet. This isn't your business." Satan said, taking a shot and sinking it.

"The hell it isn't." She said, trying to shrug off Loch, who had taken her arm.

Viper knew that his brother was looking out for him, for family, for the first time since that morning when he had asked about the girl who's name he'd said in the hot tub.

"Loch. Get her upstairs. She doesn't need to be here for this." Viper growled, taking another shot. "I'll be upstairs soon Betty. Don't worry."

“Yes. Viper will be escorting me upstairs so I can make sure he turns off all his little cameras before we have our fun.” Satan said with a laugh that made Viper want to smash his face into the table.

“Viper, no, please. I want to stay.” Betty pleaded but Loch scooped her up and carried her out of the room.

“Are you sure your brother isn’t going to use his dick to distract her while I kick your ass?” Satan said, lining up his shot.

“Nah. Loch knows better than to mess with what’s mine.” Viper said, praying that he was right.

It wouldn’t be the first time that his older brother betrayed him, Viper hoped that whatever connection Loch had with Betty was enough that he would want to give her what she wanted, time alone with Viper, more than he wanted to fuck her.

Neither of them would ever force anything from her, their father made sure that there was no chance any son of his would ever use force on a woman. They could beat, maim, and kill any man that crossed them, but a woman was something to be protected. For all his talk Satan had been raised better too. Every man in that room knew his mother had been treated as a goddess up until the day she died in

Samuel's arms.

"And you know better than to mess with what belongs to me, Viper." Satan growled, sinking another ball.

He did, but he didn't regret for a second helping that girl get out of town, change her name and everything about herself that she could. He would do it all over again in a heartbeat, even though it had meant losing his best friend of more than a decade.

"Maybe she wasn't as 'yours' as you thought she was. Ever think of that?" Viper asked with a scoff.

Shot after shot they traded barbs, threats, and general insults. Both were careful not to go too far, almost as if there was a small part in both of them that still loved the other like a brother that they hoped would one day return to the family.

It came down to the final shot. Viper knew that if he missed it, Satan wouldn't. This was the last chance he had, not only to spend the night with the woman he needed like nothing else he could remember, but to open the door to mending things with Satan.

If Satan fucked Betty things would never get fixed between them because if he took her and left, then Viper would have to kill him to get her back. If that happened Viper would be a dead man walking until the Dukes brought him to

Samuel for execution.

He had to make the shot. Every eye was on him and they all knew what he wanted.

Exhaling slowly Viper drove the cue forward, a hard, crisp thrust that sank the eight ball in the left center pocket.

“Fuck. You lucky bastard.” Satan said with a growl.

“Yeah, that’s how we do it, Viper.” Ox said, clapping his hands together.

Viper had his eyes on the door to the kitchen, but Loch still hadn’t appeared, which meant he was upstairs with Betty.

“Come have a drink and celebrate, Viper.” Rex and Dev called from the bar where Doc was busy pouring shots from a mason jar.

“We got shine for just such a victory.” Doc said, cheerfully sliding the glasses to the front of the bar where Blades was ready to light them on fire.

“Drink up boys. The girl can wait a few more minutes.”

“Maybe she can.” Viper said, laying the cue on the table and slamming back the rest of the whiskey in his glass. “But I can’t. Goodnight gentlemen. Satan.”

With a nod to the son of the club president, who was silently heading towards the bar, Viper left them all behind and thundered up the narrow staircase to knock on Betty's door before shouldering it open.

Betty was sitting on the bed, in the fluffy black robe from that morning and smiled at him with relief in her eyes. Loch was sitting on the floor by the bathroom, his feet kicked out across the floor, a beer still in his hands.

"You won?" Betty asked, getting to her feet, and walking towards him.

He noticed that her hair was wet and looked at his brother. "You two have a shower? Feeling better than you were downstairs?"

He didn't want to think that Loch had been up here enjoying her while he had been playing for her safety. The thought of her luscious curves covered in soapy bubbles, washing over her like cream, was appealing, as was the vision of her hands running all over her body, working the soap into a lather. It all had him as hard as a rock in his jeans, but the idea that Loch's hands could have followed hers sent a spike of jealousy through him that was dangerous so soon after he nearly lost her to Satan.

"No man." Loch said, getting to his feet. "I'm as dry as a bone and so's my beer after watching that lovely little shower show that our girl Betty just put on for me."

"Show?" Viper asked, stepping inside, and shooting a look at Loch that was a definite command to leave the room.

"I wanted to wash the feeling of Dagger off me and Loch didn't want to leave me alone. He sat on the floor and watched me shower." Betty said, reaching out to touch his arm, pulling his focus back to her and the soft skin starting to peek out at him.

"That's all. No harm, no foul, little brother." Loch said, heading to the door and locking it behind him when he went downstairs.

20

"You won? You really won?" Betty asked him, the excitement in her voice bringing the smile back to his face.

"I won babe." Viper said, touching the tips of his fingers to the side of her face. "Left side, center pocket."

She was so damned beautiful and hopeful. Her hands on him were eager and when she reached inside his hoodie to trace around the barbells on his nipples and down his stomach to the buckle on his belt. He couldn't help the growl that rumbled out of him.

"There is so much I want to do to you. So many places I want to put my hands, my mouth, but not right now." He said, kissing her forehead.

"What? Not now? You've wanted me since I interviewed at the bar. I know that because I've wanted you just as long. Alone, no sharing or watching. Viper? Tell me that you don't want me. Tell me that I was wrong or kiss me, but don't make me wait again."

"I'm not saying that I don't want you. God knows that I want you more than I should, but you got groped by Dagger, after Satan got you so drunk you could barely stand. I don't want to take advantage of a woman who is scared and still half drunk."

He brushed a strand of hair from her forehead and groaned when her skin flushed under his touch. "Damn you're making this hard."

She cupped him through his jeans. "I want to make this hard and I want you to take me to that bed and fuck my brains out."

He took her wrist in his hand, bringing it to his mouth to rake his teeth across her pulse. "And that's how I know you're still drunk. Go to bed and sleep it off. Then, you and I will have our fun."

Viper couldn't believe he was saying this. Everything about her screamed that she wanted this as much as he did, but he had to do it right if they were going to build something real.

"You're serious?" She asked, blinking hard as she teetered on her heels.

"As a court summons." He grumbled, leading her to the bed. "I want you to finish this water and rest for an hour, then, if you're sober, I'll join you. Okay."

"Fine." She sat on the bed and drank the water he had forced into her hand.

Sitting beside her, it was even harder to resist the

temptation to lay her down and explore every sweet inch of her. He would take his time and make her shiver with desire, aching to the core. He'd make her beg for him before feeding her every inch of his cock.

"Maybe sleep isn't such a bad idea." She said, laying down and sliding her feet onto his lap, still in the heels that almost stabbed him in the junk when she settled them in his lap.

"Maybe taking these off isn't a bad idea either." He slid the strap off her heal and gently removed first one shoe and then the other.

"Oh, that feels nice." She murmured against the pillow when he started to rub her feet.

"Shh. Go to sleep." Viper said, smiling when she relaxed at his touch. "I'll be right here. I'm not going anywhere else tonight."

"Stay with me Viper. Just, here, next to me." She patted the bed beside her. "Then I know you're not leaving."

"I'm not going to leave you."

Putting her shoes on the floor before pulling his off boots and setting them beside the delicate heels, Viper pulled the mostly open hoodie over his head and tossed it to the chair across the room.

"Oh my god."

He turned to look back at Betty who was staring up at him with her jaw wide open.

“What? You’re staring.”

“I don’t think I’ve ever seen your back. Those tattoos are amazing.” She said, tracing the tip of her finger down his back.

“You can play with those all you want when you wake up.” He said, laying next to her and pulling her close to his chest.

“I’m going to play with way more than your tattoos.” She mumbled, snuggling into him with such trust he wasn’t sure how to react besides placing a soft kiss to her forehead.

“Just sleep.”

At least an hour later Viper was dozing, almost asleep but not quite, when he felt the release of his belt and fingers teasing the top of his painfully stiff jeans.

“Well hello there.” He said, his voice rough. Opening his eyes, he could just barely make out Betty’s face in the moonlight. “All sobered up, are you?”

“Mmhmm. Sober and I still want you to fuck my brains out or let me climb on top of you and ride until we both scream.” She whispered in his ear while she slid her hand into his pants to take a firm hold of him.

"I like it when a woman knows what she wants." He chuckled, thrusting his hips so she stroked him from base to tip. "Aren't you a little over dressed for what I'm going to do to you?"

"You're the one wearing pants, gorgeous." She said, craning her neck up, asking for a kiss that he was more than happy to give, now that she was aware of what was going on.

"Stand up." He ordered, guiding her up to her feet so that he could run his hands over the glittering curves hidden from sight by the robe she was still wearing.

"As pretty as you look in this robe, your bare skin is much prettier." His hands found the belt and tugged it open, pushing at the shoulders at the same time she put her hands on him.

"I've never been with a man like you, Viper. Under all these rough, hard edges, the piercings and the tattoos, you are a truly, mesmerizingly handsome, exquisite man."

Her hands were everywhere, touching his shoulders before running up to caress his head. Viper couldn't stop himself from leaning into the gentleness of her touch.

"I don't know about that, but I do know that you are the kind of beautiful that wet dreams are made of."

The bathrobe landed in a puddle on the floor and, when he ran his hand up the inside of her thigh, she was wet with arousal too.

"Speaking of wet dreams." He let his hands rest on the curve of her backside and tugged her closer, until she was so close that he could smell her. "Let me taste you."

He teased her folds, hot and wet to the touch, waiting until she bucked against him, before licking the sweetness of her from the tip of his finger.

"Just like honey. I want some more of that." He lowered his face and tugged her close enough to put his mouth on her. Drinking her core, lapping at her with his tongue as she moaned.

When her fingernails dug into his shoulders, he laughed against her, one orgasm down and many more to go. Gripping the cheeks of her ass to lift her off the floor, Viper fell back on the bed, moving her with him until she was sitting on his face. He positioned her so that she could grind her heat against his mouth, spearing her with his tongue to taste her even more intimately.

"Oh my god." She cried out, her thighs tightening on his head.

Betty must have thrown her head back because he felt her hair touching his hands where they cupped the curve of her ass.

He could feel her juices flooding his face, rolling down his cheeks onto the bed.

"Just let go baby. Don't hold back. Give it to me." He growled against her as she writhed for more.

He eased her onto her back, wanting so badly to sink into her but it wasn't the time, not yet. There was so much more that he wanted to do, to give her, before taking that last, wild, step together.

"Viper?" She called his name in a voice that had him biting his lip instead of her neck, so he didn't leave a mark on her perfectly smooth skin.

"I'm right here Betty." He said, kneeling between her legs and looking down at her.

She was spread out across the bed, her hair like a silk shadow across the stark white pillow. He ran his hands from her knees down to grip her hips, his thumbs drawing circles on the sweet lines where her legs met everything else that he wanted to explore.

"I'm going to make you shiver, Betty, baby, then I'm going to make you sweat and then, oh then you're going to scream for me."

"Okay. I like the sound of that." She answered breathlessly.

It was his turn to get his hands on her. He couldn't leave a mark on her like her fingernails had left on his shoulders and arm, but he'd be damned sure that he'd be memorable. She was going to remember this, either as the first time they were together or the only time, but she would remember.

Propping himself above her with one hand Viper cupped her breast, circling her nipple with the pad of his thumb before he took it in his mouth. Sucking her, rolling the sweet bud with his tongue until her back arched, made him smile and when he lifted his head, he got to watch her eyes clear and try to focus on him.

"Stay with me now Betty. I don't want you to miss anything."

He lowered his head to kiss her lips, forgoing the gentleness he had used when she was still drunk and going for the heat of passionate possession. He wanted to claim her, now, so that no one else would ever think of laying a hand on her without considering that she was his woman.

Thrusting, sweeping, biting. Everything he had went into that kiss and she played back with just as much passion as he was giving. Breaking the kiss to feather his lips across her cheekbone he whispered in her ear at the same moment he touched a fingertip to her clit, circling slowly.

“You look so beautiful when you’ve cum so hard you can’t see straight.” He tugged on her earlobe with his teeth. “Let’s see if you can show me that again.”

She nodded and he kissed her mouth again before setting to work at tasting and touching every inch of her body. from behind her ear, then the inside her wrists before moving down her ribs to nip along her hips as she squirmed and moaned.

He planned to work his way down her legs and back up to devour her sweet pussy again, but she grabbed the top of his jeans and sat up to put her face right against his. They were breathing the same air.

“You tasted me, now, I want to taste you.” She said with a devious smile.

He didn’t get a chance to nod before she started to tear at his jeans, tugging them down over his hips.

“Stop scratching at me and I’ll take them off.” Viper said with a laugh.

He shucked the jeans to the floor beside her robe and knelt back on the bed, stroking her hair as she looked over his naked body slowly now that there was time and privacy for her to do whatever she wanted. He fought off the urge to flex while she ran her hands over him.

“Sit down and hold on to the headboard, Viper.” She said,

her eyes lighting up.

He scoffed a little and settled back against the wooden headboard. “You’re not going to tie me to this thing now, are you?”

She shook her head and tied her hair back into a ponytail. Crouching between his legs, Betty looked up at him.

“Hold on tight. You let go of the headboard and I’ll stop.”

“Well then, yes ma’am.”

He gripped the wood tight, letting his body relax as she kissed his inner thighs, nuzzling his erection aside to flick her tongue against his balls. He groaned. The little witch was going to torture him until he couldn’t take it anymore.

The licking and kissing were getting him harder than he had been all weekend. His shaft was weeping with pre-cum by the time she lathed her tongue across the tip.

“Damn it, woman. You’re going to make me lose my mind or my control if you keep that up.” He growled, wanting to grab hold of her and end the cock-teasing games.

“Maybe that’s the idea. You’re too controlled and I want to see what happens when you let go.”

He was going to give her a smart-ass reply but before the words could form in his mouth, she slipped hers over the head of his cock and slid those pretty lips all the way down to the base.

"Holy shit." He looked up to the ceiling, praying that he could last long enough to impress her. After all the drama of the night, Satan and then way Dagger had scared her, he had to make sure it was as good as he knew it could be. Good enough for her.

She started to hum and his grip on the headboard got close to shattering the wood. The vibration, the pressure, and the suction were sending him so close to the edge he needed to take charge, and he needed to do it now.

His hands flew from the headboard to grip her ass. The contact brought her mouth off his cock with a surprised smile.

"Get that sweet sugar up here, now." He commanded, sliding her up to his lap, grinding his erection against her. "You had enough playing around? You ready for this? Really ready?"

21

"Oh yes."

She was ready, she was more than ready, and if the way he had white-knuckle gripped the headboard was any indication so was Viper. He was long, thick, and harder than he had been since the night in the bar when they met. He was hard for her and they were all alone, finally.

"Are your camera's on in here? Is Loch watching from your office?" She asked, sliding her hand between them to stroke his length. "He got a show already. I want this to be just for you and me."

"I've got the key to that room and I unplugged everything that would make watching us easy for anyone who might break in. We're all alone and, tonight, I don't want to talk about Loch and what he did or did not get to see tonight." Viper growled at her, kissing her hungrily.

"I don't want to talk at all. I want you, in me, now." Betty said, raising her hips just enough for him to sheath himself inside her at last.

It was amazing, the feeling of him filling her, stretching her, and thrusting deeper with every move they made together. She gripped the headboard to give herself some leverage to grind down harder, farther.

She couldn't believe the sensations flooding her body. Sitting on Viper's cock gave his hands and mouth the opportunity to continue the stimulation teasing he had been doing earlier. His teeth dragging across the pulse at the base of her neck made her feel so alive she couldn't keep her hands off him.

Betty caressed Viper's head and neck, then ran her hands across the rippling muscles of his shoulders and leaned in, to kiss Viper. His growl and the way he swept his tongue against hers had her moaning and wanting more. His eyes were closed but she could tell, when she broke the kiss, that he was trying to hold on to the control she so desperately wanted him to let go of.

"Viper? Open your eyes. Look at me." She begged, rotating her hips against him in a way that she knew would drive his cock a little deeper inside her.

"I'm looking baby." He said, finally opening those deep brown eyes to stare at her.

Betty smiled and leaned back, propping herself on her hands before looking down, hoping he was looking with her. Her entire body was glistening with sweat, the room felt hot, so did his skin where they touched. From the position she was in it was gloriously easy to see Viper's veiny cock sliding in and out of her body at an ever-increasing speed.

"Look at that cock of yours filling me up, stroking everything I need. It feels so good."

"You're fucking gorgeous Betty." He said, his eyes on his cock then lifting up to her eyes. "Absolutely gorgeous."

She gasped as he stroked her from the inside, but there was no time to blush at his comment, though his words made her feel as though she were the most beautiful woman in the world. When their eyes met, he finally snapped, and she got her wish. He let go of his self control.

Seconds later, Viper shifted her from his lap to her back, bending her knees to her chest as he continued to work her body with his cock, setting her up for wave after wave of pleasure. She could feel it building and her hands searched the bed for something to hold on to as she shivered.

"Getting close, Betty?" Viper murmured in her ear. The weight of him pressing against her was heavenly. She had forgotten how good it felt to have a man on top of her, easing her legs a little lower while he drove his body into hers.

She nodded, not trusting her own voice as the pressure and pleasure continued to build. Her hands locked behind his head and pulled him down for another kiss. The smell of him was everywhere, she was drowning in the scent of leather and bourbon, and she loved it.

"So close. More please…oh please." Everything in her body was ready to explode, she was so close to the edge that it was all she could think of. "Viper please?"

He must have heard her because he sped up his rhythm, his hands gripped her harder and he pounded his cock into her until she was screaming his name, bucking against him and trying to pull him as close to her as she could. She didn't want him to stop, but she couldn't hold back much longer.

"Oh yeah. Beg for me, Betty?" He purred in her ear. "Just let go and I'll give you everything you never knew you needed."

Her hands clenched the sheets, her head tipped back and everything in her body, every nerve, exploded in the kind of fireworks she had only heard about from her friends.

"VIPER! Oh my god!" She screamed into his mouth.

Her hands slid from his head to his shoulder, clawing to pull him closer, to feel his breath as he gave in to the same physical sensations. He whispered her name, over and over again, while his body shuddered. When he had emptied himself into her, he rolled to her side.

Laying between her and the edge of the bed Viper smiled

with a wink. Her heart melted at the boyish charm that she hadn't expected. His hand traced her cheek. The touch was so soft, gentle, that she found herself leaning into him.

"You okay?" He asked, flicking his tongue across his lips and drawing her attention back to him. "I didn't hurt you or anything did I? Not sore or bruised?"

"Not hurt." She said with a smile. "No bruises or anything like that. What about you? Are you okay?"

"Betty, baby, I'm so much more than okay." He said, pulling her closer. "Though I think we're upside down in this bed."

He kissed her softly, making her want more of him all over again.

"Let's get turned around. Do you, um, want me to stay? Or should I go so you can get some rest."

Betty gripped his arm as they both sat up on the bed.

"Don't you dare go. I want you to stay. I really want you to stay." She put her hand on top of his. "Viper. Stay. Sleep with me?"

He spun her on the bed so that the headboard and pillows were behind her.

"As the lady wishes." He reached to grab the discarded

blankets and settled them over both of them, turned to flick on the fan beside the bed.

Betty watched the ‘big, bad, biker man’ settle in the bed beside her. His head rested on his hand as he watched her, that boyish smile still shining at her in a way that melted her heart and her body all over again. He reached out and traced his fingertips from her neck down her ribs and back again. “So?”

“So, I think you’re amazing. I know I’m supposed to say that you’re the best I’ve ever had and stuff like that, but you’re…that was…wow.”

“You think so, huh?” He asked sheepishly. He looked at the ceiling, rubbing his jaw before he looked at her. “So, what happens now? I don’t usually sleep with girls afterwards.”

She couldn't believe that he doubted how much she enjoyed herself, enjoyed him. All the attitude and swagger from downstairs was gone and in its place was a man who couldn't seem to be able to stop touching her.

"What happens next is sleep. You, there and me here. We're going to sleep and I'm going to try not make you wake you up with a hard-on." Betty said with a teasing smile. She wanted to see that sleepy boyish smile again. It was a whole new side to him that was fascinating her. She refused to think about the fact that he hadn't mentioned anything about doing this again. She still had a few hours tomorrow to convince him that there was something more, something real.

"Well darlin', I can't say I won't wake up with one anyway and if you wanted to help with relieving that I'm sure I'd appreciate it." He chuckled warmly and tucked her body against him. She was facing away from the door now. Even though it was locked, Betty had a feeling that Viper was trying to keep her sheltered from the other men in the club, at least for tonight

"What's your name? Your real name?" She asked, resting her head on his arm instead of the pillow. "I'd like to know."

He stilled, and she could feel him holding his breath. "We don't use real names here Betty and we don't tell them to outsiders. That's how cops and other clubs find ways to dig into our personal lives."

She scoffed. "You really won't tell me? After a weekend of sex games and what we just did? You risked a lot of trouble to be with me and you still call me an outsider?"

"Rules are rules, Betty. A member can tell his old lady, or serious girlfriend, but not a bedmate."

She wasn't going to let him know that his words hurt as much as a slap in the face. "Oh. Right. Members only." She pretended to doze off, hoping she didn't embarrass herself by crying. She let the soothing rhythm of his hand stroking up and down her side relax her enough to fall asleep. She swore to herself that if he didn't want her, if he just wanted the win, then she would treat him just like the other men. No more special glances or touches. If she wasn't special, then neither was he.

Betty woke up with strong arms wrapped tight around her. One hand spread across her stomach and the other cupping a breast. For a few seconds she panicked, pulling against the hold, forgetting who was there. A sleepy voice drawled from behind her. "Shh, shh, darlin'. It's alright. You're safe. I've got you. It's alright."

"Viper?" Was it really him? She racked her brain to piece together what had happened the night before. Trying to sort dream from reality and figure out how he came to be sleeping snugly behind her, holding her like a lover.

She felt sore in all the right places, which told tell her that they had finally had sex. Had it just been the two of them? She vaguely remembered Loch being in the room, but had he been in the bed too?

"That's my name." He replied, kissing the back of her neck. "Good morning."

Those strong, muscular arms tightened around her and his

morning wood pressed invitingly against her backside. She was so tempted to turn around and take care of the erection herself when she remembered that he wouldn't tell her his name, his real name, since she wasn't his girlfriend or 'old lady' or whatever other nicknames that the club members called the women they kept around.

"Good morning." She sat up and looked from the sun filled window to the clock beside the bed. "Wow. It's eleven already? We should probably go downstairs, right? They'll be waiting?"

He sat up with her, looking a bit disheveled and stretching.

"If that's what you want, yeah, we can go downstairs. Why not dress up for serving food? The guys will love it and you'll look hot in that black silk French Maid dress on the back of the door." He pointed across the room to the closet.

"I didn't notice that last night. When did that get there?" Betty said, climbing over him to go and inspect the dress.

"It was inside the closet last night. I imagine Loch moved it while you were in the shower. You want to wear it?" He asked, swinging his feet out of bed and standing.

"Holy shit." Betty said, unable to stop herself when she saw him. Outlined by the sun behind him he was gloriously naked, erect, and delectable. She wanted to get on her knees and devour his cock or push him back on the bed and ride him hard and fast until they both came apart again. Not until he told her his name. She wouldn't give him any more of herself until she knew that she meant as much to him as he did to her.

"You like what you see? Because so do I." He said with a grin, curling his finger at her. "Come on over here and we can play a little more."

"I like. I like a lot, but I think I have a business arrangement to honor downstairs. I'm a woman of my word even if you do look good enough to eat." She pulled the dress off the hanger and walked over to him. "Dress me up like a doll and we can go downstairs to play with all the other children."

22

He wasn't sure what he had done, but something was different. Last night she was begging him to bed her, tell her his name, everything but actually date her, but this morning she was distant, all business and almost cold. It was like the night before hadn't mattered at all to her. He knew that it did, he'd seen it in her eyes and felt it in the way she cuddled up to him. This morning he might as well have been Ox or Loch for all she seemed to be interested.

"Well come on over and I'll dress you up for the boys, though I gotta say I like what you're wearing now an awful lot." He said with a teasing grin that made her smile back at him.

After he pulled his jeans up but before he fastened them, he slid the dress over her head and spun her around the lace up the back. He pulled her against him, pressing his erection into the crease of her ass.

"You sure you don't want to take a little time? I know I'd enjoy keeping this private time going just a little longer."

"I think that we made them jealous enough yesterday and I can smell coffee." She said, grinding back against him, just hard enough to tease him. After last night he knew that he wanted more of her.

Viper knew he was going to be the one to drive her home in just a few hours and when he did, he was going to do whatever he could to make sure he got the chance to keep her for himself.

“I don’t want to stand between you and your coffee but damn it, woman.” He turned her around to face him. “I’d rather have you for breakfast than anything they’re cooking down there.”

She smiled and reached up to connect her fingers behind his head, pulling him closer.

“You want me for breakfast?” She asked with a smile that made him think of all the utterly wicked things she could do with those lips.

“I want to eat you up, drink you down, however you want to spin it. I want you, right now.” He growled. Lowering his head to kiss her possessively he dragged his teeth across her bottom lip and gripped her ass with both hands. “I want you.”

“Yeah, you and everybody else in this building.” She said, kissing him back and stepping back to adjust those oh so perfect breasts to sit higher in the dress.

He could see the edge of her nipples barely hidden by the lace around the neckline. The guys were going to go crazy for her in this, but the idea didn’t thrill him as much today as it would have yesterday. Was he already starting to think of her as his own? Was it supposed to be this way?

"Well I'm the only one who got to sleep next to you all night. No matter what else they did or get to do before I take you home, I get to claim that one."

She was slipping her feet into a pair of heels but paused and looked up at him.

"You? You're driving me home?" She asked, her hand on the doorknob.

"Yeah. I drew the lucky straw for that one." Viper replied, pulling his hoodie back on and zipping it half-way up so his chest, that Betty liked to stare at, touch, lick, was easily accessible for her sweet lips or hands.

"Yeah, lucky." She said quietly before leaving the room.

He followed her down the stairs, confused as to what changed overnight. The cheers from the members at Betty's appearance brought a smile back to his face. She was waiting at the bottom of the stairs and when he rested his hand on her hips, she leaned against him like the attention she had been so eager for was now overwhelming to her.

"Just remember they all want you, almost as much as I do." Viper said before going to get some coffee and pouring a cup for her.

"So, Betty. I think this morning, as a really nice farewell, you should serve breakfast to the table in that pretty little dress you're wearing." Blades said, taking a long drink of coffee and raking his eyes over every inch of her.

"Alright. I can do that if you fellas want to go sit down." Betty said, stepping forward out of Viper's reach. "Breakfast will be served momentarily."

"Loch has everything ready for you to bring out." Blades said, snapping his fingers at Viper. "You'll be joining us in the dining room, lover-boy, no distractions."

"You got it man." He said, waiting until the only ones in the kitchen were Betty, his brother, and himself. "Fuck. He wasn't kidding about things last night, was he?" He asked Loch, who was still at the stove, wearing an apron for a shirt.

"No. You dumbass. You pulled some shit last night that Blades can't ignore. You're lucky Satan didn't ask for your ass on a platter because he would have had to give it. Get out there and don't fuck up. They might still let you drive her home. If you're fucking lucky." Loch said, pointing towards the door. "I got her in here."

Viper looked at both of them and he was relieved to see that there was some worry for his safety on Betty's face.

"I got this. He can't blame me too much, I hope." He said,

ducking out into the dining room, which was silent as the door swung shut behind him.

"You made a hell of a statement last night Viper." Blades said, making sure that he saw that there was no chair set for him at the table. "I'm going to ask you again, are you staking a claim to that woman?"

"No. I understand that she is here under contract to the club until I drive her out of here in a few hours. She's not mine."

The words were killing him, and he was glad that Betty wasn't there to hear him say what he knew was a lie. She was his and he'd be sure to make that clear to her as soon as he could.

"So, you stepped between a senior member and hired pussy because why?" He asked.

Viper felt his hands tighten into fists but did his best to keep his voice calm.

"Because he scared her, and I made a promise."

"You made a promise? To the party favor?"

He could have sworn that Blades was trying to make him slip and let his temper and his claim on Betty show so he could really punish him.

“I keep my promises. It doesn’t matter who I made it to. That was more urgent than anything Dagger wanted to do to her.”

“You’re going to prove that she doesn’t mean anything to you. Stand at the door and watch breakfast, silently.”

He nodded. “Alright. No one is going to hurt her. That was my word to her.”

“Trust your brothers here and keep your hands to yourself.”

Taking his position by the door and opening it when Betty approached with a tray of food, Viper prayed that he could pass this test. If he could get through today, then no one would ever touch her again because she would be his.

He watched as she served the food to the five men at the table, each of them enjoying the torture they were putting him through as they put their hands on her. He couldn't move, couldn't react. When Ox pulled Betty into his lap and kissed her, his big hands wandering over the curves that had been pressed against him only hours before, he did nothing but blink. He refused to give them the satisfaction of a reaction.

He knew they would all congratulate him tomorrow if he told them that she was his but today, today they would punish him through her and they would enjoy every second of it because there was nothing he could do about it. There could be no payback for tugging down the lace collar and taking each of Betty's beautiful breasts into their mouths and suckling until she threw back her head to moan with pleasure.

Yesterday he would have been able to say for certain that she was putting on a show just for him, but today she was barely looking at him. It wasn't until she was sitting on Blades lap, feeding him off his plate like a Roman slave girl that Loch finally came out of the kitchen.

"You're a fucking idiot."

"So you keep telling me. What exactly makes me an idiot today?"

His brother leaned against the door frame opposite him.

"Your lack of skill with women for one thing. Also, the way you manage to go from club favorite to woodshed trouble in about thirty seconds. He said, shaking his head.

"This, coming from the guy who can't manage to get a girl or his patch?" Viper retorted.

"Hey, I had Jade."

Viper scoffed, his eyes on Betty and Blades, who was obviously trying to get him to react by tugging Betty's top down until her tits were on full display and in his hands. That's when her eyes locked on Viper's and he knew that she was thinking about his hands on her.

"Yeah. You had Jade and then you lost her to the same shit I saved Betty from last night. If you want to keep a woman then you have to keep her safe." He smiled. "Handsome man saves me from the monsters. That's what Betty said she needed and that's what I did." Loch shook his head. "Sweet fuck..."

He jerked his head to the table where Dev was placing a breakfast sausage in Betty's mouth, her lips closing around it the same way they closed around a cock. Once her lips were locked around the meat he started to pour the syrup. It rolled from her lips, down her cheeks and neck to pour over either side of her bare breasts. Coating them in the sweet, sticky, liquid.

"God, I'd love to be cleaning her up right now." Loch said, adjusting his jeans with a groan. "I'd have her ride my dick while I lick those gorgeous tits clean.

" "Seriously?" Viper growled. "Shut up. That's my woman or will be." Loch looked at him

"You better be careful how loud you say that. You know what Blades will do if he hears that and you know we're going to share her a few more times."

Viper glared at his brother. "The hell we are."

"You know she likes the three-way man. The way her eyes light up when we give her a few dicks to choose from tell us that. The girl is kinky and likes variety. Are you going to take that away from her? You know you're not."

Viper smirked to himself and nodded. "Yeah, and it's better with you than anyone else in this place."

Loch grinned. "Finally, something we can agree on."

He held out his fist and Viper met it with a chuckle. The resolution and agreement with his brother made it a little easier to watch the other members pass Betty from lap to lap. They weren't fucking her, just making a snack out of her chest and neck.

As the meal wrapped up and junior members arrived to do the clean-up, Viper began to worry that Blades might call for a train on her. There would be nothing he could say or do.

Sharing her in a threesome with his brother was one thing but watching five guys fuck her while he watched might be more than he could tolerate now that he knew how much he wanted her for himself.

"Well gentlemen, after that hot lunch with sweet Betty here, I think there's only a few things left to deal with for the weekend. Unless any of you have business to bring to the table?"

They all shook their heads and Ox helped Betty off the table.

"Loch. Take the young lady upstairs to get cleaned up. Then maybe for a walk." Blades said dismissively, his eyes fixed on Viper.

Loch gestured for Betty to join him. "You got it. About an hour?"

"That should do it." The senior member said, his voice growing serious.

Viper patted her backside as she passed him and shot her a wink that made her smile before he turned to face the men around the table. He was pretty sure that he knew what was coming and, either way, this wasn't going to be fun.

"Viper. You know that Dagger is a senior member and Satan is the son of the president."

"I didn't do anything to Satan except beat him in a game of pool." Viper interrupted.

"A game you had no business entering." Blades countered. "Luckily, he's not the one calling for your head."

"What? Dagger wants to have a go at me? As if he would stand a chance bare knuckled against me." He scoffed and shook his head.

"Oh, you're not going to be fighting back, boy." Dagger said, stepping out of one of the offices. "In fact, I'm not looking to get with you at all. That girl upstairs owes me a party between those sweet thighs and I aim to have her."

"Not gonna happen. I told her she'd be safe. You're not safe." Viper glared. Ox stood up to join him and he knew why they'd sent Loch upstairs.

"Either you take me upstairs to Betty or stand there and take a beating. Ox can hold you back if you can't control yourself." Dagger said with a smirk, stalking towards him.

"You think I'm going to let you anywhere near her? You're crazed."

"That may be so. What'll it be? Your blood or her on her back?" Blades said, stepping between the two men.

"You know the answer already." Viper growled. "Ox won't need to hold me back, just hold my hat and hoodie."

Cracking his knuckles, he stripped off the shirt and tossed it along with the ball cap to his friend.

"Bring it on, old man."

23

Once they were alone upstairs, Betty showered and dried her hair. The syrup hadn't been fun to get out, but she had done it.

Coming back into the bedroom, she took a deep breath and looked at Loch.

"What do I not know that I should? Is he really in trouble because of me? Because of Dagger?" She asked him, walking up to the bed and take the towel from beside Loch.

"Yeah. He's in deep shit but not as deep as Dagger will be when the president finds out what he did." Loch said, handing her the few things that she had brought with her and the luxurious lotions and shampoos that had been bought for her. "Take those with you too. They smell good on you."

"Oh, thanks for these." She smiled and put them in her bag. "How much trouble is he in? Should I talk to someone? Tell them that he was just keeping me safe, that Dagger scared me?"

"Well you could." Loch said, picking up the bag and heading towards the door. "It wouldn't be a good idea though and could make things worse for him. Just come on a walk with me. Out in the trees and away from all this stuff."

"They're talking to him right now, aren't they? Can't I do

anything to help?" She asked, following him down the stairs and towards the back door.

"I'm going to put his in his truck and go for a walk Betty. I was told to take you with me. Are you coming or am I forcing you?"

She looked back over her shoulder towards the door to the main room then back to where he was holding the door open for her.

"I guess I'll go with you. I don't want to make it worse."

"Good girl." He said with smile, setting her bag inside the big black truck that she guessed had to belong Viper. "Now, let's go check out some scenery."

He took her by the hand and led her into the trees. He seemed to see a path that she couldn't and before she knew it, they were in a clearing, surrounded by spruce trees and bright blue sky.

"How do you know about this place? It's beautiful." She asked, turning around to drink it in.

"Not as beautiful as you look in it." Loch said, grinning at her. "That's a damn cheesy line, but it's true. You look amazing. No wonder Viper's got you under his skin."

"Hardly. He won't even tell me his name." She looked up at him "I'm guessing you won't either?"

He shook his head. “Not mine to tell babe. I brought you out here for something else.”

Her heart stopped and she looked around. The quiet beauty becoming sinister in seconds. “Am I in trouble too? Did I… are you going to…”

“Am I going to make you scream? Am I going kiss you? Pin you against the tree over there, hike that sweet little dress up over your hips and fuck you until you can’t see straight? Yes. Yes, I am. Do you have a problem with that?”

Betty looked towards the tree then back to him and shook her head.

“I have no problem with that, with you.” Betty said, a smile spreading across her face as Loch stepped towards her.

“No problems? Good.”

He grinned and reached out to take her by the waist and kiss her hard. When she opened her mouth there was no time to think, or breath, he was there, drinking her in.

Instinctively she wrapped her legs around his hips and her arms around his neck. His hands were on her hips, sliding to grip her ass cheeks beneath the dress, hoisting the cotton up high enough to give him access to what he wanted.

She remembered the size of him in her mouth, the salty sweetness of him when he shot down her throat. That thickness buried in her was going to be breathtaking. Rubbing, stretching, throbbing deep inside her. She moaned into his mouth at just the thought of him.

"Someone's eager." He chuckled, pressing his forehead against hers while he eased her back against the tree. "Viper always has the best taste in women. Glad he doesn't mind sharing."

"Sharing?" Betty gasped, trying to focus while Loch brushed his hand across the neckline of her dress, kneading each breast in turn until she pressed her head back against the tree.

"More please." Her hands were trying to find the top of his jeans. "Loch, I need more." Between last night with Viper, and now, this, with Loch, there had to be something more between them than just the contract. Why did she feel for both of them? She wanted Loch, in her body, but Viper, she needed more from him than sex and it didn't make sense.

"You're going to share me?" She asked, trying to find her voice again.

"Don't worry about the sharing, not today. Right now, you're all mine. Little brother can have you to himself tonight." He grunted in her ear. "He won't mind what we're doing so don't worry that pretty head."

Before she could answer he was biting her neck with just enough pressure that it wouldn't leave a mark, but she would still feel it for hours. All the other thoughts in her head, besides how good he was making her feel, were gone.

"That's it. Just give in and feel. Don't worry about anything else. I've got you and you can trust me to make it feel good, baby." Loch said, lifting his head from her chest to look her in the eyes.

His eyes were the same warm chocolate brown as Viper's but there was a detachment, from the moment, from her, that his brother didn't have.

"I trust you." She whispered. "Make me feel everything, Loch."

His eyes sparked, she must have said the right thing because the next thing she knew he had undone his jeans and sheathed himself inside her.

"Oh fuck, Betty." He groaned against the base of her neck.

He was hard, thick and driving into her with a fiery intensity that was leaving her breathless. She felt weightless and heavy at the same time while he filled her. One hand holding her in place by her hip and the other slapped against the tree next to her head.

He was everything she wasn't supposed to want, every

mistake she had every considered, wrapped up in a package of rippling, sweating, muscles. She pulled his shirt up, over his shoulders so that she could look at his tattoo covered torso while he thrust into her, deep and hard.

There was only so much her body could take and his hands, mouth and cock pushed her to the limit. The pain of the tree scratching at her back increased her pleasure in a way she hadn't expected. That combined with the pressure between her legs had the tension and ecstasy building. She felt like she was flying.

"Loch, oh my, Loch, Oh God!" She cried, her head back against the tree.

"That's my name, don't wear it out babe." Loch chuckled in her ear before kissing her again. "Scream for me, come on and let it out. You know you want to."

He was right and she wanted to fight it, to not give him the satisfaction of being right but he was too good, too skilled with that giant dick, there was nothing left to do but give in to the physical sensation of a core shuddering orgasm.

"LOCH!" Her voice echoed his name to the trees, and he roared his own release a few strokes later.

He wrapped his arms around her a few seconds later, gently removed her from the tree, and eased her back to her feet.

"You're a good girl and a helluva woman, Betty." He said with a devilish grin as he took her hand. "Now I really should get you back to the truck. Viper should be ready to take you home now."

"Will I see you again? Any of you?" She asked while they walked the path back to the truck.

"Oh, I think you can count on that." Loch winked and left her by Viper who was leaning against the side of the truck.

"Thanks for looking after my girl for me, brother." Viper said, standing to face her. The sight of him made her jaw drop.

He had been in some kind of fight, but there were no marks on his hands, just his face. The slight redness on a few spots on his chest said he had been hit there too.

"What happened?" Betty cried, rushing up to him and cupping his bruised face in her hands. "Why?"

"Get in the truck and I'll get you home, okay?" He said, wincing before he opened the door for her to get inside.

Following his command, Betty ignored the gruffness of his tone until they were clear of the compound and on the road back into the city.

“Why did you get beat? Who did it and was it because of me?” She asked, turning to face him.

“That’s club business and it’s done now.” He replied, glaring at the road until she put her hand on his thigh.

“I don’t care. I want to know. Whatever that means, whatever that takes. I want you to tell me.”

“The only way that happens is if you’re my girl. No more parties like that, no more sharing you with the other members.” He looked at her as though he expected her to protest because she had just been with Loch, who had assured her that Viper wouldn’t mind him.

“If that’s what it takes, and it goes both ways, I don’t want to share you either. I’m in.” Betty said, sliding across the seat to be as close to him as she could. “I’m your girl.”

“You’re my girl?” He asked, pulling over to the side of the road and rolling his seat as far back as it could go.

“I’m your girl. If you want to…with Loch…I’m open to that and I think he wants it too, but I’m yours.”

She climbed into his lap, straddling his hips, and bending to kiss the words tattooed across his chest. Toying with the barbell through his nipple she stared into the warmth of his eyes and felt as though, beyond the bruising, she could see a bit of his soul.

“Now, tell me who beat my man?” She ordered, tapping her finger against his nose as though she was scolding a child.

“They said it was either Dagger got to lay a beating on me, or he got to fuck you.” Viper admitted. “I couldn’t let that happen. Handsome man saved you from the monster.”

His words sent a wave of horror through her, but at the same time a warmth and security that he would do that for her before they had made any statement about being together. He was a good man beneath all that rebellion and attitude.

“You did that for me?” She asked, unfastening his jeans then looking up into his eyes.

“I told you that I’d make sure you were safe. I kept my promise.” He said, touching her cheek gently. “You’re my girl.”

“I was with…you know I was with Loch, while that was happening to you.” She said, stroking him from base to tip, watching his expression to see how he would react.

“I know. That’s his way of looking after you too.”

“I didn’t want to hide anything. No more secrets.” She said. Her eyes locked to his while she slowly worked him inside her pussy. She couldn’t help the wince as he stretched her further than even the night before. It felt like making the declaration that to be together was making him harder and bigger than winning the pool game had.

"No more secrets." He shifted his hips in an upwards stroke. "Just a hell of a lot of sex and fun and we will see what happens next."

His hands were on her hips, helping her to bear down and take him all the way to the hilt. It was so amazing to be filled by him, inch by swollen, pulsing inch.

"Oh my God, that's so…"

He pulled her head down to kiss her, deeply, showing her the depth of his passion with every stroke of his tongue.

Their hips rolled together, stroking every pleasure primed nerve while his hands slid up and down her back.

"You are so fucking beautiful." He growled, his hands tightening on her hips when she dragged her teeth across his pulse.

"You're damn fine yourself." She said, her head rolling back so her hair poured down her back.

She gripped the flexed muscles of his shoulders while he pounded his cock deeper and deeper inside her. The waves of pleasure were coming closer and closer together.

"Oh God." She cried. "I'm cumming. Oh God, Viper, I'm cumming." She cried, trying to hold on to something as she came apart on top of him.

He stopped her with a finger across her lips and a smile on his.

"Blair. My name is Blair."

The Ride Continues in 2021 with "The Dukes of Hell Book 2: Loch"

About the Author

Born in Hardisty, Alberta Monica developed an undeniable love of reading at an early age. Homeschooled during her primary years, her mother not only taught the basics to her five children, but she also read to them at least twice a day. From Anne of Green Gables to Tolkien's Lord of the Rings the stories and the people behind them instilled a love of the written word.

As soon as she could hold a pencil Monica began to write her own stories. Her first complete work was 'Monkey Millionaires' in which a pair of monkeys became millionaires by selling ice cream. While it was a huge hit among the kids in the neighborhood it was just the beginning. After discovering the TV show Spartacus, and full immersion into that fandom, Monica was disappointed to find there was very little fiction to satisfy her desire to indulge a love of Roman era romance. The spark was then lit to write the stories she wanted to read herself.

Despite some eye-opening experiences (it's not as glamorous a profession as the movies would have you believe) she would not change her journey in the slightest. When she is not working or writing, Monica is a single parent to a little girl. Nothing makes her happier than when her daughter tells her that she wants to be a writer, "Just like you, Mommy." So, to keep inspiring a very special little girl, and to bring some elements of romantic Rome and the romance of real life to some not-so-little girls, she is pleased to be writing as M. Francis Lamont and brings you "The Champion's Prize" the first of her centurion saga and many more stories to come. She encourages everyone to "Live with Passion. Live with Purpose. And most important of all, Never Lose." Welcome to the beginning of something wonderful.

The Ride Continues in 2021 with "Loch: The Dukes of Hell Book 2"

CPSIA information can be obtained
at www.ICGtesting.com
Printed in the USA
LVHW081555120822
725815LV00014B/1083